D1603619

THE GOOD SIDE OF BAD

The Good Side of Bad

Beverly Olevin

WHITE RIVER PRESS
Amherst, Massachusetts

WHITE RIVER PRESS
P.O. Box 3561
Amherst, MA 01004
www.whiteriverpress.com

Library of Congress Cataloging-in-Publication Data

Olevin, Beverly.
The good side of bad : a novel / Beverly Olevin.
    p. cm.
ISBN 978-1-935052-35-7 (pbk. : alk. paper)
1. Brothers and sisters--Fiction. 2. Financial crises--Fiction.
3. Psychological fiction. I. Title.
PS3565.L447G66 2010
813'.54--dc22

                         2010020394

Book design by Marc Olevin
Text set in Minion Pro

Beverly Olevin
Visit my website at www.beverlyolevin.com

Printed in the United States of America

First Published: September 2010

For my father, Morrie Bernstein,
who faced all life's blows
with humor and optimism.
My energy for life and my creative zeal
came from you.

Being your daughter was a great gift.

After the kingfisher's wing
Has answered light to light, and is silent, the light is still
At the still point of the turning world.

—T.S. Eliot
from *Four Quartets*

WINTER
2008

Chapter 1

FLORENCE

DAY TURNS INTO NIGHT at four in the afternoon, but it's not easy to see the moment when it happens. In the winter, the sea and the sky are the same shade of gray without any horizon line between them. The moon pulls the tide out along the banks of Puget Sound. I'm sitting on South Beach in Discovery Park, waiting for the perfect light. I come here with my camera once all the people are gone, to find the pictures I have in my mind. Once the water recedes, the seaweed and shells lie still in the sand and rocks. I switch the setting on my camera that turns off the color. My photographs are black, white, and grey…the colors of Seattle in the winter.

The small world around my feet composes itself for me. My camera looks for perfect stillness. I click the shutter over and over, but I can't find the image I want. It should be perfect. There's no wind. The light of the full moon is bleeding through the clouds in the air, so soft after the rain. I wait.

A great blue heron lands on a rock not twenty feet from where I stand. His elegant long neck casts a faint shadow on the water. When he turns his head, his yellow eyes look right at me. If he will only stay in this proud attitude, I can capture him with my lens. As

3

the camera clicks, he spreads his powerful wings and takes flight, so graceful and free in the air. How I wish I could fly with him over the dark water.

I walk the beach, looking down for my pictures. There are so many here if you know where to look. I find five or six that I think will be good. Then I point my camera along the shore line and shoot the fusion of sand and sea.

It starts to rain again. I pull my parka tightly around my thin body and climb up the path that leads out of the park. I can't wait to get home and see the images I have caught in my camera.

After dinner I curl up in my bed and look at the pictures on the display screen of my camera. I'm pleased to find some beautiful rock compositions that I can print in the morning.

But then, I'm confused. There's a picture of the shoreline I remember taking. I wasn't alone. There was a man in the distance, looking directly at me. But that is not what I see in my camera now.

In my photo the beach is empty. The man is gone.

Chapter 2

PETER

A PHONE RINGING at 2:00 A.M. is rarely a good thing. It jolts me out of a sound sleep. The machine picks up but the volume is off. I figure if I ignore these unexpected intrusions in life, they will eventually resolve themselves or become someone else's concern. I don't like drama, and a middle-of-the-night call has drama written all over it. I turn over and fall quickly back to sleep.

I wake again as the morning light slides through my blinds and creeps up my body. The blinking red light on the phone reminds me of the two o'clock call. A shower first, and then I'll listen to the message. I let the hot water stream down my back and legs to take out the soreness from yesterday's run. I'd done ten miles. Not bad. The snow was still fresh on the ground in Central Park. I love running in New York in the winter.

I flick on CNBC to check the market while I have a cup of coffee. All these talking heads pontificating about where oil is going to go next, shouting over one another. They're all so eager to get their opinion heard. Like America is waiting for their every word. I don't pay any attention to what they have to say. That's not the important part. The thing that turns me on is the crazy excitement

THE GOOD SIDE OF BAD

they all have. The adrenaline they pump out every morning. Better than coffee to get me going. We're all playing the same high stakes game. I'm jazzed and ready to hit the office.

Twelve hours later, sitting at my desk at Lambert & Hall, I lean back in my chair feeling fantastic. I've put another great day under my belt. I rub my flat stomach with pride. Not bad for a guy in his forties. The hedge fund I represent is an easy sell and my commissions are off the wall. *Off the wall.* That's the expression the brokers are yelling to one another on the floor. Poor bastards. Brokers have to get up hours before the market opens to make their cut. My clients don't want to hear from me until they are having cocktails. I am a late-in-the-day money guy. It's all coming together so well I can barely remember a time when I had to struggle to just pay my rent.

Then I remember the phone message I never got around to playing. How important could it be? I hadn't gotten a panic call all day. Whatever the crisis was, it had clearly passed without my help.

I go to my weekly poker game uptown. A bunch of the sales guys and traders get together, have a few drinks, and swap stories about the day's victories. Having the best "get" of the day is more important than winning at poker. It isn't just the dollars of the sale but the balls it took to get it.

I GET HOME AFTER midnight. The blinking red light on the machine stares at me when I get into bed. No one calls on my land line. I give everyone the cell or the office. This phone is only for outgoing calls. I don't like people being able to get hold of me at home.

Don't push that button, I tell myself.

WINTER

What the hell, push it. Just push delete.

I hesitate.

Push play. Push delete.

I weigh the two options. Life is perfect. Pushing the button has the potential to screw things up. There is a third option. I flip on the television and catch the last of Letterman, turn over and go to sleep.

The light continues to blink.

Another day passes and still I choose to not listen to the message and not erase it. This middle ground feels comfortable. I am not being irresponsible, just prudent. I will wait to see if anything further happens to change my mind.

The blinking goes on. On the third day I can't look at the damn thing anymore. I have to hear the message waiting behind the light.

I push the play button. The voice is both calm and urgent, the message short.

"Your sister jumped off a bridge. I need you to get out here."

Chapter 3

SARA

I DRIVE ACROSS the West Seattle Bridge. What if Florence had jumped off of this bridge? It's so much higher than the Fremont Bridge. She could never have survived the fall from here. I glance down at the water below. The wind is kicking up white caps, making the usually calm Puget Sound look like open water. I think of Florence, standing at the edge, then purposely climbing over the top of the rail. Then the moment when she let go, allowing her body to fall. The huge black SUV next to me honks. I'm shocked back into the moment and realize I have veered into the next lane. I look over and see a young woman in the driver's seat. She gives me the finger. There are bridges everywhere in Seattle. This city is squeezed between a lake on one side and Puget Sound on the other. You can't get anywhere without crossing a bridge. Will I think about Florence every time I drive across one of the bridges?

When I got the call from the Emergency Room, I didn't wait to hear details. I just got in my car and rushed to the hospital. She was alive. That was all I needed to know. Getting that call was terrifying. I ran through the corridors looking for her until I was stopped by a doctor who told me Florence would be fine. They were running some tests and I could see her in an hour. I should go to the waiting room and they would call me when she was back from x-ray.

Jumping off a bridge was pretty bad, but I've learned from too much experience that Florence would have some explanation, if not strictly logical, for what she'd done. I am completely over my head when it comes to understanding my younger sister's behaviors.

When she got out of the hospital two days later, she went back to her apartment as if nothing had happened. She wouldn't allow me to ask her about it. Then she called and, without giving me a reason, she said she was coming to stay with me for a while.

I arrive at the market, Whole Foods. Coming here is always the high point of my week. I love Whole Foods. I was waiting at the door when they finally opened in Seattle. It's an oasis of gentle civilization. The fruit cries out to be caressed, to be admired, even loved. I pick up a perfect peach and roll it around in my hand, letting the soft fuzz tickle my palm. In the middle of winter there are these wonderful summer gifts flown in from somewhere in South America. Contemplating a salad requires a slow promenade along the produce aisle overflowing with arugula, endive, red leaf lettuce, shiitake mushrooms, and a row of greens whose names I don't recognize.

Living alone usually requires that I visit the frozen foods aisle with its lovely single dinners of crab-stuffed puffers and dill-crusted lamb crops. But tonight I'm cooking for Peter. I haven't seen my brother in almost three years and I know he's only here because of Florence. This isn't a social visit, but that doesn't mean I can't make him a decent dinner. I'll bet he hasn't had a real home-cooked meal in ages. Forget his fancy New York restaurants. He can eat just as well in my home. I'll give him the perfect Pacific Northwest dinner. I push my cart over to the fresh fish counter and carefully consider how I'll prepare wild-caught Coho salmon. I don't bother getting creative cooking just for myself, but cooking for others is an adventure.

As I drive home, I mentally run through all the ingredients to be sure I've gotten everything I need for the recipes I've selected for tonight. I arrive home, put the groceries away and go upstairs to make one of the guest rooms ready for Florence. I make the bed with my only set of single sheets. They are still crisp and fresh, even though they have been sitting in the back of the linen closet for years. On the wall opposite the bed are the three framed pictures of flowers in different shaped vases that I painted right after the divorce. Anyone with taste would probably look at them and be embarrassed for me for having had the audacity to frame such amateurish pieces. They're in identical antique silver frames, which make them look even sadder. The frames are grand; my poor little paintings could never be equal to them. It's a good thing that no one ever comes into this room.

I smile at my unschooled brush strokes and crude composition, remembering the pleasure that creating them had given me. Why had I quit painting? It wasn't like I planned on displaying them on the living room walls.

When Roger left me five years ago, our couple's therapist had told me to get a hobby, as if Roger had been a hobby and now that he was gone I needed to replace him. What kind of hobby, I'd asked naïvely. My life had been teaching third grade, taking care of Roger and our big home. The therapist cavalierly replied, I don't know, most people collect something or make something. I obediently followed his advice, went to the art store, bought acrylic paints, brushes and canvases. I filled my evenings painting the flowers that sat in pots on the back porch. I was surprised how much I loved it. But then I wish I had also realized back then that I could define the word "hobby" more broadly. Why couldn't dancing with men have been my chosen hobby?

Suddenly I'm exhausted. I sit on the bed, not caring that I am messing up the quilt. What have I been thinking? Where did I get the idea that this was going to be a pleasant family reunion? Florence jumped off a bridge and I'm cooking dinner and making beds. Peter will think I'm an idiot.

I can't decide if I'm looking forward to seeing Peter. It's not like we're estranged. We talk to each other about once a month. He feels obligated to keep me updated on the life of our mother, Mary Ellen. And I feel he needs to hear about what Florence is doing. Ironically, we rarely talk about our own lives unless he needs me to listen to one of his crises with the women in his life. Our conversations mostly focus on the lives of others.

When we were children I worshipped him, even though his greatest pleasure was tormenting me. I remember the winter when an ice storm kept us locked in the house for a week. I had just turned six and Peter was eight. I followed him around the house asking him questions to entertain myself. Can your fingers break off if they get too cold? Why doesn't Aunt Nellie have a chin? He would tell me to leave him alone.

Then one night he came into my bedroom and said he had an adult secret to tell me. "God gives every person on this earth just so many words, and when you use up all your words you can't speak any more. At the rate you are going, you'll use up all your words before you get to be ten years old. Then you'll have to be silent the rest of your life."

I was terrified. For the rest of the week I barely spoke a word. When the storm broke and we were allowed to play outside again, Peter confessed that it was just a joke. I wanted to kill him.

Then there is Florence. I have no idea what kind of mood she will be in. Things could blow up between her and Peter. They're oil and water. I'm the one she thinks of as family. At least that's the way it used to be. The truth is Florence and I haven't had much of a connection for the last few years. Talking to her on the phone is usually a frustrating one-way conversation, with me asking all the questions and her giving me one-word answers. She doesn't have any interest in asking me what is going on in my life. Not that I've had much to report, even if she did ask.

I go downstairs to start preparing dinner. At least it will just be Peter and me tonight. Florence isn't coming over until tomorrow morning.

When we three are together it will be my job to keep things civil and manageable. That's been my job for most of our lives, and I'm good at it. It's what I do in the classroom.

I help children get along.

Chapter 4

PETER

I LOVE THAT MOMENT when the wheels touch down and you know you are finally safe, part of the earth instead of part of the air. I hate flying. It gives me the feeling of impending doom. Just getting out to Seattle was a challenge. Maybe it's the loss of control that freaks me out, being thousands of feet above the ground, in the hands of pilots who might have had a few drinks earlier that night or had their stock portfolio tank that day. Or maybe some fanatic is hiding explosives in their pants. Flying is unpredictable, unnatural and risky.

I leave New York as little as possible. The other guys who sell hedge funds in the office are actually excited to get on a plane to somewhere far away, taking twenty-four-hour flights to South Africa or India. They come back exhausted and jet lagged for days. I don't get it. It's a waste of money and time. We have what they want, so why not make the client come to us? These guys are always after me to go with them. Some of them even see it as a great perk and add days on to their trips to be tourists. In the end they don't bring in any more accounts than I do staying right at home in New York. Besides I could never get on a plane with any of them. What if I had one of my anxiety attacks in the air? God, they would all think

I was so lame, being afraid to fly.

Rain. Why does anyone come to Seattle in the winter? The greyest city in America. Depressing. The natural place for my two sisters to spend their lives.

I pick up a Ford Taurus at Hertz and drive to a hotel near the airport. Staying with Sara would mean doing breakfast together and endless talking. Besides I would never get any work done. I'll do the good brother thing: show up and get out as fast as possible.

SARA IS MAKING DINNER when I arrive. Her hair is pushed back from her face. She's wearing an apron. Christ, I thought, I can't remember the last time I'd seen a woman wearing an apron. Blue with delicate flowers—it's ridiculous. The apron is the most attractive item of her clothing. Shouldn't it deserve more protection than the old jeans and baggy sweatshirt it covers? I'll never understand Sara's sense of how things should look. I watch her carefully cutting vegetables into equal-sized pieces. When it comes to salad, she is a perfectionist. Her own appearance is of far less importance to her.

When had Sara come back east to see our mother? Was that the last time I saw her? That must have been at least three years ago. She looks different…older. She doesn't take care of herself. I hate to think it, but Sara looks like an old housewife minus the wife part. She's two years younger than me but it feels like we're a generation apart. I pride myself on being trim and fit. Young women take me for early thirties. They would never guess I'm forty-two. Though we are alone in Sara's home, I feel oddly embarrassed by her. Even our mother, Mary Ellen, does a better job of keeping herself up, and she's pushing eighty.

"Florence is coming here tomorrow," Sara says, offering the knife and a cucumber to me. Helping her prepare food is always a risk. Getting it right by Sara's standards is tricky business.

"Why is she coming here?" I ask.

"Where else has she got to go? You want her to come to New York and stay with you again?"

The *never ending year* is how I remember Florence's most recent sojourn in my life. "Time for the big city," my little sister had declared.

After living in Connecticut in a fixed-up barn behind our mother's once stately farmhouse, Florence got on a train and showed up in Manhattan. I opened my door to her, hoping that her year of doing nothing had finally gotten to her. She was ready to market her college degree in music, break out her deep jazzy voice, and make something happen for herself in New York. She wasn't a kid any more. She was a twenty-five year old woman with a college degree.

I moved my home office into the living room, giving her a temporary bedroom. The weeks passed and Florence sat at the kitchen table doing crossword puzzles. Okay, I thought, she needs some time to get her act together here before she hits the streets looking for work. I'd never done much for her over the years so I figured maybe now it was my duty to put a roof over her head. If only the roof had been all that she needed!

Weeks stretched into months. I got used to coming home to empty pizza boxes and clothes all over the apartment. Kicking her out wasn't an option, as she had no place to go, not even back to the barn. Mary Ellen had long ago given up any interest in the mother role, if she ever had any in the first place. Having her youngest off-spring still hanging out in the barn was never her idea of how she planned to spend her senior years. What she wanted in the barn was a riding horse. At seventy-nine she still fancied a good trot in the country. The minute Florence left to live with me, Mary Ellen tossed in a few bales of hay and an aging quarter horse.

It was now two years since Florence had landed on my doorstep saying she needed a place to crash for a few nights. She had showed up with one suitcase and left a year later with one suitcase and my MasterCard maxed out. What she needed now was to get a job and pay me back the money she owed me, Not that I needed the money. It was just the principle of the thing. Sara had told me to let it go. "You're her brother. You've got to let family slide on loans."

I didn't see it that way. It wasn't a loan. It was a withdrawal without permission. Basically, it was theft. Florence had never been very good about money. It wasn't a real thing to her. It wasn't about the money; I wanted her to take responsibility for her actions.

She still has no job, no money and no plans. I have no sympathy for her scattered life. I'd gotten my act together in my early twenties and had made a fortune before I was thirty. I expect no less of Florence. She is wasting her gifts and throwing away a chance to build a career. She has turned into someone I don't know and don't much like.

So now she's coming to stay with Sara. Good. She could be Sara's problem now.

"She's never staying with me again," I tell Sara. "That ship has sailed. We haven't spoken to each other in two years."

"That's my point," Sara says.

"So doesn't she have any friends she can stay with? Has she burned everyone she knows?"

"That's a little cold. Peter, she's your sister. Try to show a little compassion."

"I'm a very compassionate person," I say, smiling.

Sara puts down her lettuce spinner. "Compassionate? Please!"

"I'm here aren't I? I grabbed the red-eye from New York when I got your call. I dropped everything, which, you need to know, is not an easy thing to do. Financial relationships have a shelf life of about ten minutes. You've got to be on the client all the time. Leave the arena for a few days and they move on to someone else."

"Okay, Peter, I get it. And just to be clear you didn't jump on a plane when I called. I didn't hear from you for three days."

"I'm here now. Stop chopping and tell me what is really going on. When did all this happen?"

"Two weeks ago."

I'm confused. "Two weeks ago? You said it was an emergency and I needed to come now. You waited over a week to call me! And then you get pissed off that I didn't call you back right away. None of this makes sense. Why the hell am I here?"

I toss all Sara's perfectly cut pieces in the bowl, throw in the lettuce, grab the cup of dressing she has spent at least ten minutes mixing, pour a liberal amount on the salad and carry the bowl to the table. "This salad is done. The first course is served."

Sara follows me and sits down, defeated by my greater will.

"I didn't know what happened until the night I called you. I still don't really know what happened. All I know is that she jumped off a bridge."

"Maybe," I say.

"What do you mean maybe? This is not a thing that has a maybe. Either you jump off a bridge or you don't."

"Nobody saw her jump," I argue.

"They saw her get out of the water."

"Maybe she was going for a swim."

"In ice-cold water, in the middle of winter, in jeans, a wool sweater, and a full-length coat?" Sara says, finally topping me.

"Okay, not going for a swim," I say dryly. I look at Sara's turned-down mouth and gather that she isn't going to let me lighten the situation.

This was only the most recent destructive act on Florence's part. I had been getting Sara's phone calls for over a year. I'd learned not to take any of it too seriously. I was too busy swimming upstream in the financial world to give any of my little sister's attention-grabbing behavior much credibility. Most of it turned out to be pretty risk-free. Jumping off a bridge left her with no significant injuries. No broken bones, not even a twisted ankle.

"You said she's fine."

"According to the guy who helped her out of the water she was in great shape. She actually swam to the shore," Sara says.

"Still wearing the coat?" I laugh. Sara doesn't.

"Is that going to be the level of your concern? Because if it is, I can do this alone."

"Just an observation. How does a person not get dragged to the bottom by a heavy coat? You're a teacher. You've read about Virginia Woolf."

"I guess she got it off in time."

"Not a very committed act of suicide."

"Did you tell Mother about Florence?" Sara asks tentatively.

"Are you kidding? She hardly remembers who Florence is anymore," I say flippantly.

"That can't be true," she says.

"She's old. She forgets things," I say, wondering why I'm making excuses for Mother. Mary Ellen would never bother making excuses for herself.

"Like forgetting one of her children? She's not that old."

"We aren't cheese, we don't age at the same rate. We agreed years ago: I do the heavy lifting with Mother and you get Florence. It's a division of labor."

At the time I thought it was a great bargain for Sara. Florence was doing well in school and basically it was okay to be with her. Whereas Mary Ellen could manage to pull off being judgmental and indifferent in the same sentence. I was clearly her favorite and in many ways her only child. Sara had given up trying to have anything resembling a real relationship with our mother long ago. They hadn't talked for years.

My Blackberry rings. Sara stares at me, her eyes imploring me to not answer it. I take it out of my pocket. The phone identifies the caller as Ted Anderson. After weeks of calling, this guy was finally calling me back. Ted is a big ticket and if he is ready to bite…I weigh my options. Take the call and piss off Sara or leave it and miss what could be a shot at a hot sale. "I've got to take this."

"Please don't. You didn't pick up my message for three days. We're in the middle of a crisis here. Call them back."

"It'll just be a minute. I'll take it upstairs."

I COME BACK to the table smiling, "God, he had a million questions."

"And you had a million answers."

"Actually, Sara, no, I didn't. Half the time I don't have a clue what I'm selling these guys. These funds are a mess. They've stuffed in so many small banks and security firms with impenetrable financial statements that it's all too complicated for anyone to understand. I just tap dance my way through it, tell them the returns are unbelievable, it's all secured, and they buy it."

"So why don't you tell me what to buy if it's all so safe? If you can make all this money for other people, why not for your sister?"

"I sell funds to large companies with tons of money, not to ordinary people."

"I'm ordinary?"

I laugh. "Yes, and I mean that in a good way. I would never put your savings at risk. I don't sell or even give advice to family or friends. That's where I draw the line. I can always lose as much as I make for these investors."

Sara picks at her salad. The lettuce is dripping from my liberal dressing. In silence, she takes her plate to the kitchen, tosses the contents into the salad spinner and runs the whole thing under cold water. Then it goes back on her plate and she returns to the table. She drizzles her homemade dressing on it, giving me that teacher-look that says "this is how it's done." In response, I calmly take her dressing and pour more on my own salad.

Nothing. No reaction.

When we were kids, it was so easy to tease my sister. I played on her innocent, gullible nature. She took everything at face value. Assumed that people would be as earnest and sincere as she was. Oddly, that is what I still like best about her. She isn't glib or witty and she certainly isn't New York. She is down-home family. She had always been that for me. Whenever things were shaky in my life, Sara was my anchor, the only person I could honestly talk to about the things that really mattered. Every time another relationship went up in flames, I could bitch about it to Sara. She was supportive, kind and simple – basically everything I don't want in a woman. I wanted bright, edgy, unpredictable, adventurous. But when I needed family, Sara was it. That's the deal with family. I don't have to call Sara regularly, sometimes I don't talk to her for a month. It was just a thing I take for granted.

Sara pulls a beautiful-looking salmon from the oven. My sister is a raving Martha Stewart in the kitchen. The salmon comes with a dish of exotic wild rice with crumbly things that might be cheeses or nuts on top. Then more side dishes appear, all delicious. No one has ever cooked like this just for me.

We eat in silence for a while. Food like this requires silence. Words would distract my mouth from concentrating on the sensations rolling around my tongue. Sara is pleased that her efforts and her culinary talents are being appreciated.

"So why did she do it?" Sara breaks our comfortable silence asking this simple question as if I might have an answer.

"What?"

"Jump off a bridge."

"Florence loves drama. Loves the attention it gives her," I offer. "Life just doesn't provide enough for her so she has to create it. It's like she wakes up in the morning and thinks what crazy thing can I do today? What self-destructive thing can I do that will bring strangers to my aid and my family to their knees?"

"Bridge-jumping is not normal behavior."

"It was just some kind of statement. Performance theater. The whole year she leeched off me she never once seemed unhappy or depressed. I swear she even seemed to get high off the worst things happening to her."

"I want her to see someone who can tell us what's happening to her. She was my baby. I *was* her mother. At least I loved her like one. She was my only child. I never got to have another."

"Was? She's not dead," I remind her.

"Was," she says. "I can't touch her anymore. I don't have the slightest idea what goes on in her mind. She does seem happy but in a light, unreal kind of way. Like the happiness is a dress she puts on over the child I used to love."

"Again, past tense," I say.

"It's hard to love her. Most of the time I can't wait to get away from her."

"It wasn't an attempt at suicide. Not a real one."

"She could have died," Sara says.

"You said it was the Fremont Bridge? Correct me if I'm wrong, but didn't you tell me that the Fremont Bridge is a canal bridge?"

"Yes, but it's not the size…"

"You said it's about thirty feet high. That's like jumping off the balcony of my apartment. Or diving off the high board at the pool."

"Into 42-degree water," Sara reminds me.

"More forgiving than cement."

"You're pretty calm about all this."

"Would you feel better if I panicked?"

"Maybe," she says, finally giving me the smallest hint of a smile.

We finish dinner and I flop on the sofa. "What you need is some new furniture. How old is this thing? All of this stuff? This living room looks like early Salvation Army."

Once the money started coming in large enough amounts, I

had offered Sara money for the down on a new house in a better neighborhood. She had refused, saying this was all she needed. I wanted to help her. She wanted help that didn't involve money.

"I'm broke," she reminds me. "All I got in the divorce was this house which has not just one but three mortgages on it."

"Is that even possible?" I say laughing, but Sara is dead serious.

"I had to put on a new roof and redo all the plumbing. Where was I supposed to get the money for that?"

"You've got a job."

"Right…a schoolteacher. Third grade…public schools," she says, as if this explains all her financial problems.

"You're smart. Why don't you get a better paying job?"

"Because I like teaching. I like the kids. They like me," she says, defending herself.

"God, what simple lives people live out on this coast."

"I'm simple…you're rich... you could help her."

"I've been down that road."

"Peter, I know you would loan *me* money if I asked?"

"Absolutely," I tell her. "You're responsible. You'd even cut back on toilet paper to pay it back, which I would not ask you to do."

"Responsible. That's me. I can't even imagine doing anything the slightest bit crazy. Do you want some coffee?"

"Sure."

The coffee arrives with a piece of homemade apple pie. Sara sits down next to me.

"Peter," she says. "If you didn't think this was serious, why did you come?"

"On the odd chance that I could be wrong."

Chapter 5

SARA

FLORENCE ARRIVES AT my house at nine in the morning looking like a colorful pack animal. Her arms are full of shopping bags and loose clothing, which fall piece by piece all over the floor. Under her sopping wet coat she is wearing a red tie-dyed kimono. I greet her with a hug.

"I'm here," she proclaims like a delighted child at a circus. "I still have your key, so you don't have to make me a new one. I'll come and go and you'll never know I'm here. This is going to be fun. Sisters having pajama parties. Like we're kids again."

"We never had pajama parties," I say, following Florence around picking up the clothes as they fall.

"Oh, wait," she says, grabbing several of the bags from me as I'm trying to put them away. "I brought you the best gift. It's in one of these." She searches through the contents of a green book bag. "Not this one." She tosses it aside and begins to dive into a huge white Nordstrom's bag.

"You don't have to give me gifts," I protest.

"Then it's not for you," she taunts me, holding the bag above her head as if I should try and reach for it. "It's for me…so I don't have to see you in those dull clothes any more. Clothes aren't for the person *wearing* them. They're for the people *looking* at them." She drops the Nordstrom's bag and picks up a small make-up sack, peeks inside then tosses it on to the sofa. Then she continues searching through the rest of the bags on the floor.

"Well, then, I've got nothing to worry about because nobody is looking."

Florence abruptly stops her frantic searching and stares at me. "*I'm* looking," she says. "Am I nobody?"

"No *man* is what I meant," I explain.

"Practice with me and then maybe a man will show up." She looks suspiciously at me. "So is a man showing up?"

"Who?" I ask.

"You know who," she teases me, and a little piece of the child she used to be shines through her eyes.

"Oh, you mean your brother. I don't count him."

"As a man?" she laughs. "He works so hard at being a man, a big Wall Street macho guy, he'd be mad at you if you didn't count him."

"Yes, he is coming over," I say, doubting my own words. He was supposed to have been here at eight. It doesn't matter, I tell myself. I can handle Florence. Peter might just make the situation worse. It was probably a mistake asking him to come help me. His first priority is always himself. But now, watching my little sister bounce around the room, I feel like I need Peter.

"I thought he didn't want to see me ever again," she says.

"Sure he wants to see you," I say without conviction.

"We had a terrible fight. He kicked me out of his house," she says as if this act of kicking was part of a child's game.

"That was years ago. It's all water under the bridge." The second the words are out of my mouth I realize what I said.

"Good one." Florence laughs so easily that it makes me laugh too.

"Poor choice of words," I say.

"I'm starving. Let's make some breakfast," Florence says, running into the kitchen.

She opens the refrigerator and starts pulling out everything. Orange juice, milk, eggs, cottage cheese, mushrooms, avocados – it all gets tossed on the counter. Plates, bowls, silverware, glasses, a spatula. Within seconds my kitchen is a mess. When she returns to the refrigerator and starts pulling out more foods at random, I stop her, telling her to go unpack, I'll make breakfast. She ignores me. The contents of the refrigerator are her only focus. Out come mustard, mayonnaise, tomatoes, celery, anchovies, and the remains of last night's salmon dinner.

"Stop! What are you doing?" I say.

"Making breakfast," she gives me a broad smile. "You're not the only cook in the family. I'm going to make us a bodacious omelet."

She cracks eggs and tosses them into a bowl and then smashes a carton of cottage cheese into the eggs. Florence stares at the mixture she has created, and abruptly loses interest in the whole project. She skips out of the kitchen and starts looking through her scattered collection of bags.

"What happened to breakfast?" I ask.

"Guess I'm not hungry anymore. I bought you something," she says. "It's here somewhere."

I toss the contents of the bowl into the garbage disposal and put everything back in the refrigerator.

"Look, here it is! I brought you this," Florence says, pulling out a tie-dyed low-cut shirt. "Try it on."

"Where did you get that?" I ask. "Some flea market? Tie-dye. What's that, about fifty years old?"

"It's back in style. Everyone's wearing them," she says.

"Not me," I say.

Florence's eyes narrow and in a blink the bouncy mood is gone, replaced by a tone of steely insistence. "Try it on."

"No, I'm not wearing that," I protest. "It would look ridiculous on me."

"Yes, you are wearing it," she says, roughly pulling my shirt off and forcing me to put on the tie-dye. I try to resist but decide to be cooperative. Florence's sudden mood change takes me by surprise. It's like having an unpredictable Labrador retriever in the house. One minute the dog is sweet, kissing your face and offering you its stuffed toy. But if you so much as touch the toy, it turns on you growling, showing its teeth.

Where is Peter? I think. Why is he so late?

Just as quickly, Florence's bouncy mood returns.

"There, perfect," she says. "Go look at yourself in the mirror. You don't look gray anymore."

"I looked gray?"

"Always gray," she says giving me a sad, pitying look. "Your face is gray, your eyes are gray, your skin is gray, your hair…."

"My hair is blonde," I say, wondering if that is still true. Grey creeps into my hair so slowly that it's hard to notice when blonde is no longer in the majority.

"Outside blonde," she assures me. "But inside it's gray. You need color…light. Your *blood* is gray."

She takes my arm and stares at it as though she could look through the veins to the blood beneath. "See. Grey. You need to make red blood. It needs to come up through your body to your face."

I don't know what to say. How can Florence not know how weird all this sounds?

"Is this another one of your crazy things?" I say carefully, hoping not to provoke another sudden mood change.

"No, this is real. It's science...real medicine." Florence explains the science while walking her body up into a perfect yogi headstand.

"See, this brings blood to your brain. Makes the gray matter red. Bright. Alive. Try it."

I am impressed. The kimono falls to the floor and her strong, lean leg muscles reach up towards the ceiling. Maybe I'm getting this all wrong. Maybe Florence is fine and there is some logical explanation for the bridge incident.

Her legs drop gracefully to the floor. "Now you try it."

"I can't stand on my head," I say.

"Yes, you can. It's easy." She demonstrates. "Look, you just put your head in the palm of your hands, like this and walk yourself up." She jumps up, pulls me down to the floor, helping me copy her moves. With a little effort I'm surprised to discover that I can almost do it.

"Practice, you'll get better. I'll teach you. It'll be fun." She's excited to have me on the floor with her. "We'll do yoga every morning."

"For how long?" I say, falling clumsily back to the floor.

"An hour or so," she says.

"No, I mean how many days?" I ask. "How long do you plan to stay here?"

"Do I have a time limit?"

"Of course not," I say, feeling guilty that I would even suggest that she's not welcome in my home as long as she wants to be here. "I'm just asking what your plans are."

"I don't make plans." She says it as if I have just offended her.

"You say that like plans are a bad thing. You have to think about the future."

"The present is enough for me right now," she says, moving frantically from one yoga position to another, as if she is in search of one point where she can be still. It is a chaos of movement evoking more a feeling of dizziness than the peaceful sensations that I think yoga is supposed to provide.

When Florence was three or four years old, she could sit quietly for hours and listen to me read to her, and not just at night as she was going to bed. She would come to me in the middle of the afternoon, a book in her hands and say "please read this one to me." She loved mythical stories about fantastic places full of colorful characters.

When she got older she could entertain herself for hours reading. Even as a teenager she loved to read. I remember her small body curled up on the floral sofa turning the pages of *Wuthering Heights*.

There is no trace of that peaceful girl in the person springing about the room now.

I get up my courage to ask her the burning question. "Are you going to tell me what happened?"

"My roommate kicked me out of our apartment. Just like Peter did. I'll get another place soon, real soon," she says cheerfully.

This isn't an answer to the question I'm asking, but at least it opens a door.

"You had a fight?" I ask.

"No, of course not," she says. "I don't fight with people."

"Then what happened?" I push on.

"I freaked her out. She says I scare her," she laughs. "Isn't that ridiculous? I can't scare anyone."

I sit down on the sofa. "You scare *me* sometimes."

"How?" she says sitting next to me. She takes my hands and holds them tightly as if we are about to share a very serious secret.

"I don't know. The things you do...the things you say. Sometimes they don't make sense," I say.

"Not everything has to make sense," she drops my hands with relief and laughs again.

"When are you going to tell me about the bridge?" I ask. "Why did you do it?"

She runs back to the kitchen. "What happened to breakfast?" she calls.

"I threw it away," I say, following her.

She takes a carton of orange juice from the refrigerator and drinks directly from it.

"I thought you said that Peter was coming over this morning?"

"He is," I say.

"He hates me," she says.

"No," I say, pouring the rest of the orange juice down the drain and tossing the carton.

"Yes, I think he actually hates me," she says.

"He may hate the things you do but he doesn't hate you," I say, wondering how much truth there is in my words.

"People *are* the things they do…what else can you be? I am the person who does things, that's how you know me."

"That's true," I say, trying not to sound like a teacher. "But people are more than what they do."

"No, that's wrong, Sara." She is defiant. "That's wrong!" Arguing with her seems like a bad idea. I want to get her on a more positive track.

"You are also what you think and feel," I say. My reasoning only makes her angrier. She puts her face right next to mine and explains her feelings to me as if I'm a six-year-old child.

"No, think and feel turns into DO. Think and feel are the ingredients that go into the cake…DO is the cake."

"Where do you come up with these things?" I say. "This is what I meant when I said sometimes you don't make sense. If you do a few bad things it doesn't make you a bad person. Florence, do you think you're a bad.…"

"I'm not Florence," she says with delight.

"What?" A cold chill goes down my spine. I have no idea what she's talking about. I suddenly feel afraid to be alone with her.

She sees my reaction and laughs. "Don't freak out, this isn't a crazy thing. I just don't like Florence, never did. It's an old-fashioned name. Nobody my age is named Florence. Mother was so old when I was born she gave me an old name…I changed it. I'm Chandra now."

"You were still Florence when you called me three days ago and told me you were going to stay here."

"I haven't had time to make it official. All my papers still say Florence…my driver's license, my insurance.…"

"You have insurance?"

"I'm still on Peter's policy. Can you believe that…he didn't cancel me?"

"Do you want me to call you Chandra?" I ask.

"Sure, that's my name," she says. I relax a little. Florence is making perfect sense right now. There is nothing wrong with changing your name. And she is right, it's an old-fashioned name. I would've changed it myself if I'd been stuck with it.

"I should have killed Florence a long time ago," she says. Just when I thought that we were on safer ground, she knocks me back again.

"So was it *Florence* who jumped off the bridge?" I ask, not ready to hear the answer. But I need a rational explanation. Did my sister actually believe that she could throw the old Florence part of herself off a bridge and be reborn as this new Chandra person? Or was this some New-Age ritual?

"Oh, I get it," Florence laughs. "Like I'm a split personality or something? Good one. No, it was me, Chandra…we're the same person. I'm not crazy, Sara."

"Still, you *did* jump."

"Yep."

Chapter 6

PETER

IT TAKES A MINUTE before I'm awake enough to remember where I am: a nondescript airport hotel room with a king-size bed. Ever since Lydia left me, I have been sleeping on the sofa in my office at home. I guess that Sara would think this was the sad result of a bad breakup, but I don't see it that way. The sofa is comfortable and the right size for one person. It also has the advantage of being six feet from my desk and computer so I can be on top of the rapid changes in the market.

The morning is getting away from me. One day and I already miss New York. Lydia had wanted to travel. Go to Venice, Budapest, Beijing. Why? The center of the universe is in New York. Everything you could possibly want is in easy reach.

It's hard being away from my office. I need to be part of the action. This being on the West Coast is throwing off my timing. The other guys would already be looking at mortgage loan products packaged into opaque bundles of securities and getting ready to sell them to the Chinese. In just one day I can miss maybe a half a million in sales. It isn't even the money that's the turn-on. Just getting the sale…clinching it. No one at Lambert & Hall can get them to bite like I can. I call it candy. I give them the sweet taste of the deal first with a single ridiculously high-yield security and tell them it's risk free. Once they swallow the sugar, the rest is easy.

The ticker runs across the bottom of the screen on CNBC. The Dow is taking a dive, down over a hundred points. I listen to the talking heads yell out their predictions. It all makes no difference to me. Everyone at the top of the food chain is making money.

Out here I'm temporarily out of the action, but I can still make my own trades. I want to get a few in before stocks start back up and I miss the window. What can I buy or sell before I have to leave for Sara's?

When I first began working at L & H, I had been religious about not playing the stock market myself. Other guys in the office had become addicted to the adrenaline charge and traded their own accounts right at their desks. I knew better. I believed that Wall Street was like Vegas. You could easily get seduced by all the money moving loosely around you. After a while it was nothing to toss a few thousand down on the spin of a wheel. I was a reasonable man making more money than I ever dreamed possible and I wasn't planning on putting it at risk. Let others gamble in the market. My first bonus went into the down payment on a 2,000 square-foot co-op apartment on the Upper West Side a block from Central Park.

After a few years of watching my colleagues rake in small fortunes, I decided that the Vegas metaphor no longer made sense. Stocks weren't a gamble but a sure thing if you knew what you were doing, and I figured I was as smart as or smarter than the next guy. And when Lydia left I had all that free time at night.

Trading was fun and the profits were so quick and tangible. I promised myself that I would be disciplined. If a stock went down more than twenty percent I would sell and never look back. If it went up twenty percent, again, sell with no regrets even if it went up ten percent more. This was a conservative system. I was a successful, responsible trader. Each week I took out profits and bought myself a reward for my cleverness. Simple things at first—cameras, flat screens, cashmere sweaters. Then, as the size of my trades grew, bigger treats: a Porsche, a Lichtenstein, a time-share upstate. I began to feel that I would run out of things to buy long before I ran short on profits. I was swimming in a river of easy money.

The hotel phone rings. That could only be Sara.

"It's ten o'clock. Where are you?"

"Is she there yet?" I ask.

"Yes. You promised to be here before she arrived. Why don't you just stay here? You don't need to pay for a hotel. I thought you flew in to help me. It would really help if you were here."

"Okay, I'll just grab some breakfast and come right over."

IT IS RAINING AGAIN, gray and bleak.

Room service arrives and I take my time drinking coffee and reading the financial section of the Seattle paper that comes on the tray. What a worthless rag I thought, missing the *New York Times*. Maybe I could get one down in the lobby. If only it weren't raining I could kill some time going for a run.

Maybe I'll pick up some Stoli on my way over to Sara's. Seeing Florence again is going to be hard enough without alcohol, and Sara never has anything to drink.

Why is all of this happening? I try to remember when Florence was young but I have little to draw on. I was seventeen years old when she was born, just going off to college.

Florence was a crazy afterthought on the part of our mother, who was fifty-four when she conceived with the help of a team of highly paid doctors. I never got the point of it. Mary Ellen never wanted to be a mother to her first two children. My best guess is it was a clichéd late middle-age crisis. She was fighting the clock—refusing to age—proving to herself she was still young enough to give birth. Or maybe that was the year she came in from the road because she thought she was too old for the clubs and she just needed something to do. Taking another shot at motherhood was something to do. Then Dad died of a heart attack, and the prospect of raising a child alone at her age wasn't in Mary Ellen's plan. A year after Florence was born, she was back out on the road singing with a jazz band, and leaving Florence to fifteen-year-old Sara, who was willing and able to play the role of mom.

I have to admit that Mary Ellen was one hell of a singer. Her deep throaty voice had Ella Fitzgerald written all over it. My father had never had the patience for jazz or children and pretty much ignored all of us, spending his life locked in the cellar building mechanical inventions that never worked.

That first year I came home from school for Christmas and spring vacations to find Sara changing diapers and feeding our little sister. A series of live-in housekeepers replaced Mary Ellen as head of the house but Sara was head of the family. When Mary Ellen came in from the road, which was becoming infrequent, she would head straight to the grand piano and sing blues to her three offspring as if they were all adults sitting in a crowded bar with a glass of scotch in one hand and a cigarette in the other.

In spite of the chaos at home, I watched from afar as Florence thrived under Sara's care. She was a bright, happy kid who could sing your socks off. At least that gene had been passed on. Over the years I showed up to watch my little sister star in school musicals. She was a show stopper, getting standing ovations with her amazing range and emotional theatrics. Florence was an "A" student and scholarships to college came easily. Then, somewhere in her early twenties, it all fell apart. She lost interest in music and started spinning in ten directions at once. When she lived with me she took up belly dancing, which seemed innocent enough, except her eyes glazed over when she undulated, making her look like a snake charmer in a trance. She was more frightening than enticing. Then she started reading about religious fanatics speaking in tongues. She practiced doing it herself. I overheard her when she was alone in her room in my apartment.

Right before she moved out of my house, I had found her meditating with her hands in ice cold water until she couldn't feel her fingers. It was supposed to isolate her from the outside world and heighten her inner senses.

Losing touch she had called it, without a trace of irony in her tone.

Chapter 7

PETER

ARRIVE AT SARA'S HOUSE three hours after I told her I would be there. Maybe that's for the best. Florence is already there, so I have managed to miss one of her dramatic entrances. Sara would have had time to calm her down and I could walk in to find them quietly having coffee.

"Glad you made it," Sara says. Her disappointment at my late arrival is replaced by her relief that I'm finally here.

"Sorry, I got tied up this morning," I say.

There's Florence squirming around on the floor chanting Om. She doesn't look like someone who's just jumped off a bridge. She looks fine. More than fine; she looks terrific. Red hair falls in soft curls over her shoulders. I try to remember what color her hair was when I last saw her. It had been blue when she first arrived at my door but it quickly went through the whole color spectrum. I remember that she was born with the same wispy blond hair that I had. In fact she had looked just like my own baby pictures, with those big hazel eyes dominating her face.

"Hi," I say trying to sound casual.

She doesn't respond. I try again but she ignores me.

"Try *Chandra*," Sara offers quietly.

"What?" I ask.

"She changed her name to Chandra. Yesterday I think," Sara explains.

"I can't call her *Chandra* after twenty-five years of..."

"She doesn't like Florence," Sara whispers.

"Neither do I." I decide the best course of action is to do nothing. "Have you got any coffee?" I ask Sara.

"Sure," she says, getting me a cup. I follow her into the kitchen. "What's going on?"

"Just talk to her. Please," Sara implores me.

"Okay." I return to the living room and sit down on the floor next to Florence.

"Hey." No reaction. "You're looking good. Thin. So, are you all right? You gave us quite a scare. We worry about you."

Nothing. I look to Sara for help but none is offered.

Florence moves into some kind of yoga thing with her hands and feet all on the floor and her butt stuck high up in the air. Then she begins to hum loudly.

"Can you stop doing that and talk at me?" I ask, as if it's a polite request.

Nothing. I ask Sara, "Is she talking to *you?*"

"Yes, she's been talking to me all morning. She's also been doing this yoga on and off for the last three hours," Sara says.

Florence doesn't move for almost five minutes. "Give her time, Peter," Sara says.

"Maybe she's meditating."

"Better she should be medi-*ca*ting," I say.

"Florence, can you please get up off the floor and talk to me?" When she doesn't respond, I feel my patience wearing thin. "Look, kiddo, I flew across the whole country to see you so maybe you can get up and talk to me."

"Call her Chandra," Sara says.

"You've got to be kidding me," I say, but Sara gives me a pleading look. "Okay, I'll play."

I sit down on the floor next to Florence, who still has her butt up in the air and her head on the ground. I wonder how this doesn't give her a terrible headache—all that blood rushing to her brain.

"So you're Chandra now," I say. "Nice name. What does it mean?" She doesn't respond. I feel like just bagging the whole thing and getting on a plane back to New York. What is the point of my being here? My little sister is a pain in the ass and I'm not going to change that. She's probably enjoying this little scene.

I try a new tack. "How about I change my name too?" I say. "I'm sick of *Peter*. He's a forty-two-year old guy, in great shape, although he is going bald. Let's see who else I can be. Maybe *Jason*. Yeah. Jason is a young hip guy. Women like Jason. 'Hey, Jason, can I make you dinner on Saturday night? Or better yet, how about I make you breakfast?' I like Jason. So—Chandra, meet Jason." Nothing.

I give it another try.

"How about Sara here? Let's get rid of her too. Let's see. I've got it. Let's call *her* Florence. You see how this works? Mom's sister was named Florence. ...She named you Florence to give her sister a new incarnation. So now this *new* Florence walks into your living room transformed into Chandra. You can see how this might be disturbing...to Mother...to us. So how the hell are you little sister?"

Florence continues to ignore me.

She begins moving into one position after another, all of them looking precarious, wobbling on one leg. I watch her. Yoga. I haven't got the patience for it. But just because it's not for me doesn't mean there isn't a lot of money being made here. It's getting bigger all the time. People are opening studios on every street corner, as though yoga is the new Starbucks. There are ads for hot yoga, cold yoga, yoga with chocolate, quiet yoga, flow yoga. I don't get it personally. Why make it so complicated? Do a few stretches and run a couple of miles. Still, when I get back to New York I should look into the big studio chains. There might be a good investment there.

Sara sits on the floor with me. "Floren—Chandra, please talk to your brother. It took a lot to just get him here."

When Florence doesn't respond, I give her a little kick, knocking her out of her yoga pose. She laughs, turns to me and smiles brightly.

"Hi, Peter," she says, as if the last half hour never happened. "What's going on?" She doesn't wait for an answer to her question. "I taught Sara how to stand on her head. I could teach you. Want to try it? It feels great. Gets you into a whole different mind state. Helps you relax."

"No, I don't need my world upside down," I say. "I'm glad it helps you. Can we talk now?"

"What about?" she asks.

"Well, for one thing," I say, "both Sara and I would like to know why you jumped off the Fremont Bridge."

"Do you really want to know or are you just asking to be polite? If you want to know, ask Mom," she says indicating Sara.

This throws Sara. "Florence, I'm not your mother."

"Look little sister," I say. "We need to know if you're being delusional or just playing with us."

"Don't use that word, delusional," Florence says with a touch of fear in her voice. "It's a real word. It means seeing and hearing things that aren't there. People say it like it means just kidding yourself. Pretending, and knowing you are pretending to yourself. Words have power. If you call me delusional it can make it happen. The word goes into my brain and my brain reads it and then it spreads through neurons to my body. You do it often enough and the body becomes *delusional*…feels things that aren't there. I'm not delusional, and you *are* my mother."

"I'm your sister," Sara says, looking confused.

"Nope, you changed my diapers and fed me."

"Like you can remember that," I laugh.

"I don't remember…I know. My body knows. If you learn to listen to your body you can see into your past. Into the future, too. Your body can see what's coming just like wolves can feel the wind and thunder coming."

I'm thinking where does she get all this woo-woo crap? Then she looks at me like she can read my mind. "Don't think that way. That's not crazy. You're always looking at me for *signs*. You're two frightened people looking at me from a safe place over the road… staring at me like I'm snow on a mountain…waiting for the moment when the snow is too heavy and the avalanche happens. That's the way you want it…safe… Not me. I'd rather be the mountain…feel the avalanche around me, through me…that's being alive."

"Here comes the melodrama," I say.

"If you don't make your life a drama, you're just walking through it. Pretty dull if you ask me. Deny it all you like," she laughs. "Sara is my mother."

"She's right," I play along. "For all practical purposes, you are her mother, Sara. You did raise her. Mom lost interest and went back on the road. Singing her lungs out at a bar or club near you this Saturday night."

"I don't sing anymore," Florence says, going into another crazy twisty thing.

I hear the rain getting stronger and see the gray getting grayer. It's like I've flown to a planet without a sun. Why do sane people choose to live here? It couldn't be a choice. Maybe, like Sara, they came here for a lover or a job and never got it together to leave. For fifteen years Sara has lived in this broken-down house with a leaky roof and bad plumbing until I offered her the money to get it all fixed. She wouldn't take my money. Instead she gets another mortgage to pay for it. I always thought she would move back to Connecticut after the divorce. I offered her a plane ticket and moving expenses, but she never even entertained the idea. She made it clear that she considered Seattle her home.

Then Florence migrated to Seattle after she left my house two years ago. I look at my sister in her yoga body, thinking, God, she looks strong and healthy.

"Chandra." I'm in the game now. "So what does the name mean? Is it some mystical goddess?"

"Signs. Always looking for signs," Florence says.

"Just want things to be clear here."

"So you want to be my brother again?" I consider whether this might be an unexpected opportunity to opt out.

"That's what I am," I reply.

"Never much."

"I was going off to college when you were born."

"And you never came home again."

"I did. I came to visit. I just never lived there again."

"I've got no parents," Florence says without emotion.

"You had Sara. Mother wasn't gone *all* the time. Look, I flew all the way from New York to be here for you."

"Why?"

"Because you jumped off a damn bridge," I say with growing frustration.

"You didn't come when I got carried away by ravens."

"Sara," I look at her for clues. "Did you forget to tell me about that?"

"She was in a play," Sara says. "Some kind of Indian myth thing… raven puppets picked her up. She's big on myths."

"They had huge beaks," Florence says, acting out the play as she describes it. "Raven brought the light to the earth before time when everything was black. The beak broke. He dropped me to earth."

"Did you get hurt?" I ask.

"Everyone gets hurt. You can't avoid it, so why try? You miss so much trying not to get hurt. It's never as bad as you think. I broke two toes, little ones. It wasn't a bad thing. I got to fly through the air for a while."

I figure she has just given me an opening with the flying thing. "Is that why you jumped off the bridge, to fly through the air?"

She ignores my question. "You didn't come when I wrecked my car," she says. "I drove it into a tree. You didn't come when I burned my hands in the fireplace. You didn't come when I swallowed a wasp. You didn't come when I— "

"I get it. It's a long list. What's the point?"

"Why are you here now?"

"Those were all accidents, weren't they?" I ask with suspicion.

"Accidents," she says. "My life is an accident. A miracle of highly unlikely events. Why are you here?"

"The bridge was pretty dramatic," I say. "You finally came up with something that got my attention. Is that what you were trying to do, get my attention?"

"Wow, somebody thinks they're awfully important. Can you control me from three thousand miles away?"

"Then for Sara's attention," I offer.

"I thought we weren't speaking?"

"Well, we are now."

"Are you still mad at me?" she asks cautiously.

"You wrecked my life like you wrecked your car," I say calmly. "And you walked away without a scratch."

"You're getting too thin," she says poking me in the stomach. "You should eat better."

I push her away. "You told Lydia I was gay!"

"She didn't have to believe me."

"You told her I brought young boys home and made out with them in front of you. You told her that she could never trust me!"

"It was a test. If she loved you enough, she wouldn't have listened to me."

"I don't know why I'm here," I say. "By the way, you still owe me $35,000."

"That was a gift, which means I'm not required to pay it back."

"Please stop this," Sara says, as she sits in the corner rocker, putting her head in her hands. "I don't want you two fighting in my house."

I turn on Sara. "What's this, Switzerland?"

"You're not helping. You came here to help, not to fight." But her soft voice steals the conviction from her words, leaving Florence and me free to ignore her.

"Sara," Florence says, "I can leave if that's what you would like. I don't have to stay here. I can find lots of other safe places to stay." She begins picking up her bags. "That's what I'll do."

Sara responds as Florence knows she will, jumping up to come to her rescue. "It's pouring out there. You can't go out without a coat. Stay here until you get a place…stay here. Why don't you go unpack your stuff? Is the suitcase and those bags all you've got?"

Florence shoots me a triumphant glance. She has played Sara off against me and won. "I travel light," she says, bouncing around the room gathering up her pieces.

"Where are all your books, your photographs, your camera?" Sara asks, trying to move the three of us to something resembling cheerfulness.

"Gave them away. It's just stuff," Florence says, as if tossing away most of what you own is meaningless.

"Your work is not stuff," Sara says in her quiet supportive voice.

"Hang on to the old stuff, you've got no reason to make new stuff," Florence says flippantly.

"You never go anywhere without your camera," Sara says.

"Left it for my roommate. It wasn't working."

I bought that camera for Florence years ago and she just gives it to her roommate. I'm about to blow up again but Sara stops me.

"I could get it fixed for you," she says, so sweetly.

Florence laughs. "It's not the camera. The *pictures* didn't work. I couldn't get things to slow down."

"That's what's great about your work. It's full of action. Even your portraits. There's always this feeling that something is about to happen. That's a hard thing to create in a still photo."

Sara could put a positive spin on acid rain.

Florence stops jumping around and seems really to consider what Sara has said. "That's not what I wanted. I wanted to click the shutter and stop everything, quiet everything. Find the one point when everything was still. No past. No future."

There is a sadness in her tone that takes both Sara and me by surprise.

Florence breaks the silence by grabbing her suitcase. "I'll stick this in the guest room. I'm a guest, aren't I?"

Sara takes her upstairs to give her one of the four empty bedrooms. Why had Roger insisted that they buy such a big house? What a waste, all this space. This house is too big for Sara. She should be in a neat little condo. I wonder what this house would go for. If the market is about to turn sour, I should talk her into selling now.

But then I'm forgetting about Florence.

Chapter 8

FLORENCE

THIS HOUSE IS SAFE, at least for a little while. No one knows I'm here yet. Peter will go away soon and it will just be Sara and me. That feels right. Sara won't push me. We will be a little family again. I can get her to do whatever I want.

This room is full of old things. Pictures of me when I was a child. Sara took them all. There are no pictures of Peter or Sara because there wasn't anybody to take them. Then there are the bought old things. Sara goes to flea markets like I do. She buys dark wooden stuff, tables, desks, chairs. Lamps with shades that have tassels. Things given away by the children of dead people. They don't want their parents' stuff anymore. They want to collect their own stuff that their children will one day give away. I don't want things that stay after I'm dead. I want to be clean and free.

They want to know what happened. I could tell them. Maybe, if I could get it right myself. That's the problem. It's like when you wake up in the middle of the night and the dream you were having is perfectly clear. You can remember every detail. But that only lasts for a few seconds. Then it is gone completely and no matter how hard you try to bring back even a piece of it, you can't. Not an image, a fragment.

Sometimes I remember but I don't know if it's the right story. And it has to be the right story for them.

Peter likes to have the facts right. I don't get it. The facts aren't always right. And what is right for Peter may not be right for me. I'll make a story for Peter that goes step-by-step with all the moments stacked neatly on top of one another.

I will say that they were following me. Three of them, the hoods of their black jackets pulled over their heads. Then I will give him a picture of me, with the collar of my own coat pushed against the back of my neck to keep out the cold night rain. Then I will make the three figures move as I move, slowing with me, quickening their pace as I do. I will tell him how it seemed strange at the beginning. He'll expect that.

Sara will want to be inside my head, knowing whether I was afraid or excited. She doesn't want a collection of events. She needs to know about the part of me that was hungry to fly.

Maybe I'll tell her what the hooded black jackets want with me, the secrets I had to offer them.

Peter will only want to know, in exact order, what happened. I'll tell him that I thought they would turn off when I reached the bridge. That I didn't look back.

I'll say that I started across the bridge. A few cars passed by, their headlights lost in the low clouds. I didn't look but I knew the three are still behind me, following me up the walkway that overlooks the black water.

Peter will want to know why I didn't look for help. I'll tell him I could have flagged down someone, asked for help, but who were the drivers hidden in those speeding cars? Maybe they were more dangerous than the figures walking behind me.

I'll tell him this: a gust of wind slapped rain across my cheek. As I got closer to the center, the span of the bridge seemed to expand. Each forward step I took lost me ground. I looked back to see that the figures had picked up their pace. In a moment they'd catch up with me. Perhaps pass right by me, laughing with one another and ignoring me.

Sara will want to know what I felt at that moment. Fear? Anticipation? It's hard to decide. I'll tell her what I felt mostly was puzzled.

Then I'll come to the end of the story, and my brother and sister will understand it all.

The figures surrounded me, smiling, touching me. I was flying through the air, light and free. No longer on the bridge but above it, sailing on the night wind.

I flew over the water, certain that I could keep myself aloft, away from the icy water below.

Someone was shouting.

I went under. My eyes popped open. I was still flying but now in water rather than air. Flying and swimming are the same. I was light and free. There was no gravity pulling me down. The air, the water, held me up. For a moment I spread my arms and legs wide and the water held me in its embrace. The moon hung in the sky above my head. I felt it swirling the waters around me. Just as the moon pulls the tides of great oceans back-and-forth, she pulled the blood within my chilling body, changing my gravity and my buoyancy.

I untangled myself from my heavy water-soaked coat and swam to the shore. Arms were grabbing me from the water. I didn't know it was possible to be that cold.

I looked up. The three figures from the bridge were gone.

Maybe.

Or maybe that isn't what happened.

Maybe I will just tell them both *my* truth. And in telling it, I may learn what my truth is.

Chapter 9

PETER

ONE MORE DAY WITH MY sisters and I can get on a plane.

After my third cup of coffee, I remember that I haven't called Mary Ellen in a week. I don't plan on telling Mother about Florence's bridge leap but I will have to explain that I'm in Seattle and can't visit her. That might be a challenge. She knows that I never leave New York without a serious reason. The only exceptions are my visits to her. She isn't going to buy a casual sibling reunion.

I pick up the phone and call her. She never says hello when she answers the phone. Usually she'll say, "Yes?" It may sound like a question the first time you hear it, but it soon becomes clear that the tone is meant to imply she is impatient to get this interruption over with. Sometimes she answers with her name, "Mary Ellen here" as if she is radioing in from a field position. This time she picks up on the fourth ring with an opening I haven't heard before, "I'm busy, is it important?" My response is always the same, "Hi Mom, it's me."

When she asks me to bring her some brandy, I mention that I'm three thousand miles away in Seattle so the brandy would have to take another week. Why do I bother worrying about her? She doesn't even ask why I'm here. She doesn't care about anything outside her small world. She tells me that the cleaning woman has stolen her riding boots.

"Why would she do that?" I ask.

"Because she wants to go riding," she says dryly, as if it shouldn't be necessary to state the obvious.

"You're getting as blind as a bat, Mother," I laugh. "They're probably at the back of your closet. It's a mess in there."

"That's why I have a cleaning woman. To put things in order, Peter, and to find my boots."

The conversation jumps from one topic to another with little to no segue. "The remote isn't broken, Mother. You probably just have it upside down again."

Sometimes I'm afraid that the old Mary Ellen is falling away. She had never wanted or needed anything from anyone before. She had been furiously independent her whole life and now she asks me for at least ten things every week. But her sense of humor is intact. We have a few good laughs and I promise to call her when I get home.

DOING NOTHING EXCEPT going from the hotel to Sara's house and back is making me feel cooped up. I need to burn some energy. Damn rain. I need to run. That's the only thing that works for me. What the hell, I think, putting on my running shoes. People who live here must run in the rain all the time, what choice do they have? How bad can it be? I run in the snow all through the winter in Central Park.

A light drizzle brushes my parka as I step outside the lobby. I remember Sara suggesting a great place to run a mile from her house. I get in the Taurus and head out across the West Seattle

Bridge. It's not Central Park, but Lincoln Park is a decent enough place for a run. I figure I'll do three or four miles.

In just a few minutes I find myself running through what looks like a forest along a bluff overlooking Puget Sound. I've got to say this is a mood changer. The air smells fresh, like salt and eucalyptus. Two guys, maybe in their mid sixties, come towards me running at a good pace. They smile as we pass, saying "great day, gotta keep the body moving." They were actually talking to me. Five minutes later the same thing happens only this time it's a young woman jogging with her border collie. Her greeting is even more surprising. "Looking strong," she says. "Have a good run."

"You too," I say, smiling back at her.

This is feeling so good I don't want to stop. I run down the path to the beach. My feet hit the ground in long strides. The repetitive movement takes over my mind, compelling me to keep going. The running is easy. Stopping is hard. Sometimes I get the feeling that I could run the whole day and still the adrenaline would keep feeding me. I hear the whistle of the ferry announcing its departure. Sara told me that the little landfall you can barely see from the corner of her bathroom window is Vashon Island. It takes the ferry just fifteen minutes to get there. As I turn on to the sand, I slow my pace so that I can watch it move out into the water. The horizon line disappears as the sky and water become the same shade of grey. I watch it until the ferry becomes a speck in the distance.

Then I pick up the pace. What matters most isn't the distance I run but my speed.

I think about my morning runs in Central Park when I feel that primal pleasure in pushing harder, going faster. The rush of pride and superiority I feel when I pass regular runners who had passed me the day before. The pleasure I feel in being unbeatable.

I look at my watch. Forty minutes on the button. I gently jog back to the car.

Not bad. I'm ready to see my sisters again.

BY THE TIME I GET to Sara's, the light rain has turned into a storm. Florence is delighted by it.

"Winter. It rains every day. Peter, I could go running with you," Florence offers. "When you get all sweaty and hot on the inside you can't even tell it's raining on the outside."

It is ten in the morning and Sara already has her apron on, her little housewife armor, ready to start cutting up stuff for dinner.

"I'm going to go shopping later. Anybody got any requests?" Sara asks.

Florence gives her sister a puzzled look. "Requests...requests... re-quests...What a strange word. Like you are taking away all your quests. The journey is over."

I opt to ignore Florence's word play. "Are you still a vegetarian or was that only when you lived with me?" It is more of an accusation than a question.

Florence gives this long and serious thought. "No longer a vegetarian...I'm a vegan."

"Oh God." I drop down onto the sofa with my sixth cup of coffee.

"Vegan, yes. That sounds right for Chandra. She will be a vegan."

I thought the name change was just yesterday's drama. "You're just deciding this now? And talking about yourself in the third person. Is that one of the signs we're supposed to be looking for?"

"Good one." She has my attention at last. "Chandra is new so she can be anything I want. I get to invent myself all over again. See first person...not crazy."

"Great. That's what we'll do today." I decide this might be interesting. "We'll invent Chandra." With Sara's white board and pens, I take charge. "Let's make a sane and responsible Chandra. What characteristics shall we give Chandra?"

Florence loves the game. "Tall. Let's make Chandra tall and thin."

"Okay, tall." I write it on the board. "Now, given that you...as Florence...are basically considered to be a person of rather short stature and that you, again, as, Chandra, are twenty-five years old and not likely to grow any more. So just how does Chandra get to be *tall* is the problem."

"Forget tall." She jumps up and erases the word from the board.

"This is silly," Sara says.

I ignore her. "What I had in mind here was not so much physical characteristics but aspects of Chandra's personality. Is Chandra happy or depressed? Is she loving or aloof?"

"Aloof. Another great word. Like something you scrub your body with," she laughs.

"That's a *loofah*."

"Peter why are you doing this?" Sara asks. "It's not helpful."

"It might be. So what do you think Chandra...happy or depressed?"

"What a choice. Happy of course."

"The problem is I'm having a hard time figuring out why you jumped off a bridge. If you were depressed, then I might understand it better."

"I didn't jump. I was pushed."

Chapter 10

SARA

A
N ELECTRICAL STORM closes the airport. Peter's red-eye flight to New York is cancelled. He is trapped with us for another day. We're having a blackout. I am prepared with candles and propane lamps. Lightning flashes, followed a few seconds later by thunder, mean that the storm is almost over our heads.

"How long is this going to last?" Peter asks, as if I could have an answer.

"If it's a local power line, they'll have the lights back on in a few hours. If it's the whole area, it can take all night," I say.

Now that Florence has gone up to bed, Peter and I can talk about the long and confusing story she has just told us. It had started off believably enough with a gang of muggers following her across the Fremont Bridge. How she had tried to stop passing cars for help. But somewhere in the middle of her story she got lost, letting mythical images take over.

"How can Florence sleep through this?" Peter paces the room.

I think he is actually scared. The thunder is like a sonic boom shaking the house. The lightning is even worse. I can see it cutting the black sky in jagged pieces. He asks if there are things you aren't suppose to touch during an electrical storm. Phones maybe. Water. Anything metal.

"Peter, sit down." As soon as this storm passes, he will be gone. I need his help now. "We need to figure out what to do about Florence. I don't know what to make of it, do you?" I ask. "What did she mean? She said she was *pushed*."

"We could choose to believe her." Peter walks to the window and stares at the storm as if it is a personal assault on his life.

"Then why are we sitting here instead of calling the police?" I challenge him. He doesn't believe she was pushed any more than I do.

Finally he comes away from the window and sits down with me. "Okay, maybe part of it is true."

"Which part?" I ask. "It doesn't make sense. Three tall men in black hoods push a girl off a bridge for no reason?"

"There was a reason. What was it she said?" He is trying to remember Florence's exact words. "'They were sent to punish me for stealing.'"

"Stealing is reasonable," I say, remembering that Florence was arrested twice for shoplifting when she was in high school. "But it's *what* they accused her of stealing."

"Souls." Peter repeats the word as Florence had said it, as if it were a musical note rather than a word.

"It gives me the shivers thinking about it." I suddenly wish the blackout was over and the lights would pop on.

"Yeah, if the black hoods of death weren't enough of a tale. The *stealing souls* thing puts it squarely in the crazy category." Peter says the word we have both been avoiding, *crazy*.

We look at each other, both of us hoping the other will find some way to explain what is happening without the word *crazy*.

"We could be making too much of this," I say. "Maybe she was mugged by a single man who did push her off the bridge. Maybe she was so frightened she remembers it in an exaggerated way."

"And maybe she's truly nuts," Peter says.

"I can't face that," I say. "I know she's done lots of crazy things but I never really thought she was truly crazy...I mean, mentally ill. What are we going to do?"

"Get her help," he says.

We sit in silence and listen to the rain pelting the windows.

PETER GETS UP AND RUMMAGES around the kitchen cabinets. "You never have anything to drink in your house. I was going to pick up something yesterday but I ran out of time. Nothing, there is nothing here. It's like being in a Quaker home."

"That's because I don't drink."

"You should. You need at least one vice to be fully human. Besides, we're in the middle of a crisis that clearly rises to the level of alcohol consumption."

"Stop trashing my kitchen." I get out a step stool, climb up and pull out an old hidden bottle of cognac. "Does this do anything for you?"

"Ah, Courvoisier. Not bad. The real Sara reveals herself at last."

"It was a Christmas gift years ago from the parents of one of my students," I say.

"Lovely, a virgin bottle. Just what we need." Peter gets two glasses and pours one for each of us.

"Not for me." I push away the glass.

"Oh come on. The apocalypse is happening out there," he waves the glass in front of me. "Give it a go."

"I don't even like the taste of liquor," I say.

"You will like this, I promise you. This stuff was invented for nights like this…also for dysfunctional families."

"Maybe I should mix it with something." I look in the refrigerator for tonic water.

"Mix something with cognac!" Peter laughs. "You really don't know anything about drinking. A taste?"

"One sip." I carefully bring the cognac to my lips and allow a few drops to slide into my mouth. "It's strong."

"Wait a few seconds and feel the chill leave your body," he instructs me.

There's another lightning flash. "What the hell." I take a big swallow and feel my face flush. I take another swallow.

"Slow down, girl. This stuff is supposed to be sipped, not chugged."

The rain is so loud we can hear it pounding the roof on the second floor. Peter rolls the cognac around in his mouth. Then puts it down and gives me a look I have seen on his face a million times when we were growing up. His mouth curves up in a tight smile and his eyes squint. It's the face he makes when he is both serious and joking at the same time. It's as though his face is moving in two different directions, not sure what his next words will be. He looks back at his empty glass and pauses for a long time.

Finally he says, "And who takes care of us?" This strikes me as funny.

"Okay," he laughs. "We've got each other."

"You're two years older than me," I remind him. "And you

smoked for years... I'll end up taking care of you. Then you'll die and I'll be back to being alone."

"Family reunions bring out the cheer in you," Peter says, starting to relax. "I have an idea. Maybe you could adopt some obedient Chinese children who will adore you and wait on you in your old age. You have plenty of room in this house. You need to fill it with life."

"Not a bad idea," I say.

"Maybe it's too risky," he says. "Putting all that work into raising kids when there is no guarantee they'll show up for you later. Children, remember, become people who you may not even like or, more likely, who may not like you. You become nothing more than an obligation, a necessary evil."

"Pretty cynical stuff even coming from you, Peter," I say. "I'd worry about you if I thought you actually meant half of the things you say."

"I mean them all, in varying degrees," he smiles.

I have spent so little time with my brother over the years. I'm glad to have this little moment to just be for us. I want him to remember who I am, to talk to me about something other than Florence's and Mother's problems.

"So what's going on with you, Peter?" I ask knowing that *he* is his favorite topic. "Have you even had a relationship since Lydia left?"

"Relationships are overrated. *Relationship,* such an imposing word. Florence is right, words do have power. A relationship is a battleship of a word."

"Let me know when you think of a better word. What about sex?" I ask, taking Peter by surprise.

"So what are you asking me?" he says smiling.

"Something about sex. Like, do you have any?"

"Sex is easy. I'm a bachelor who has a great body, an apartment with a view of Central Park, an overpaid job, and no children from a previous marriage…baggage free. I'm a catch. Women are easy to find and easy to forget. The battleship is near impossible."

"The problem is you still love Lydia. You're not open to someone new."

"I'm open, Sis. Lydia was years ago."

"So you talk to her...see her?" I ask.

"She got married in October. Florence did a hell of a number on her. Poisoned the well permanently."

"Why did Florence tell her you were gay?"

"To get rid of Lydia so Florence could keep leeching off of me," he says.

Peter pours me another cognac. I can feel it going down through my body all the way to my toes. What had I been missing all these years? Drinking feels good. When had I become such a Puritan? I was always afraid of losing control. Whenever my head started to get fuzzy, I would put down the liquor and reach for black coffee. I'm feeling fuzzy right now but I don't want this feeling to go away. Fuzzy is good. Being clearheaded is overrated. But then, I may just be getting a little drunk.

"See, I still don't get that," I tell Peter. "Why would Lydia take Florence's word over yours? It's ridiculous. She knew you weren't gay."

"Florence is a good storyteller. Remember when she was a little girl, she would make up the wildest stories and somehow make them sound true."

"You slept with the woman!" I laugh. "That should have cleared up any questions."

"Discussing my sex life with my sister. Maybe not a great idea."

"What are we going to discuss, *my* sex life? I don't have one. And since you made me drink this stuff, I'm not ashamed to say that it's something I miss…very much because I was good at it and it feels good to do the things you're good at. I had lots of sex when I was young. Do I shock you?"

"Maybe a little."

"And, as an experienced woman, I think Lydia would know after sleeping with you, that you aren't gay. Unless you're a very good actor, or maybe you *are* gay. Not that I care…you can sleep with sheep for all I care." We laugh. It feels good. It's the one thing that keeps me from flat-out disliking Peter's selfishness. He can always make me laugh.

"See, a little cognac can really loosen you up. Actually, I'm not unaware of your promiscuous past. I seem to remember an affair you had in Greece. Two weeks at the Club Med in Corfu with this hot lover. You were crazy about him."

"We use that word 'crazy' too often in this family," I say.

"What was his name?"

"I don't remember. I was twenty-two."

"Two weeks over…vacation at an end…he tells you he's bisexual….has male lovers. So same question you tossed at me. You slept with him. Couldn't you tell he was a switch hitter?"

"He went to Oxford. All those upper-class English college boys slept together then. It was a rite of passage. I don't think he was going to keep working both sides. He liked me. He liked tits."

"So do I. So we're both boringly straight." Peter raises his glass. "To tits."

"To tits." I clink his glass. "Do you remember that summer we went to Elk Lake? Mother was singing at that club all night and sleeping all day."

"Sure, that was the summer I taught you how to swim," he says.

"We spent every day in the water…just the two of us. It was the first and last time you paid any attention to me. I was ten. You were almost a teenager. You made me a little boat out of driftwood."

"I don't remember that," he says.

I get up slowly. The cognac has really gone to my head. I reach up to the top of the bookshelf and pull down the old dusty drift-wood boat.

"You kept this piece of junk?" We both burst out laughing again.

"Are we drunk?" I ask.

"Maybe a little."

"Enough of this," I say taking the cognac back to the kitchen. "This guy's going away. I'll make some coffee." Peter follows me.

"Are you really going back tomorrow? I need you here until we figure out what's happening with Florence."

"The market has been going crazy. I can't leave it hanging. I've got to be there."

I want to yell at my brother, to beg him to stay. I want to tell him I can't handle this alone, but I know it won't help. Maybe he's a coward. Maybe he does care about Florence but he'll still leave me alone to deal with her problems. The prospect of meetings with psychiatrists and weighty decisions is not his forte. I'm the caretaker in the family. He will leave me to play my role. He probably won't even feel guilty.

I think about the cognac in the cupboard. That might help.

Chapter 11

FLORENCE

'M ON THE FLOOR MOVING through poses looking for the perfect still point. *Om Namah Shivaya Gurave,* I chant as I move. I stand up into warrior pose with my arms straight out to my sides, my legs under them. I'm Poseidon, god of the sea, throwing my spear at the attackers. Strong. Powerful. That's what I am. *Untouchable.* No one is going to push me again.

Peter stumbles down the stairs in a T-shirt and boxers. The storm has forced him to spend the night. He is hung-over and pissed off.

"Christ, I thought chanting was supposed to be a quiet peaceful thing. Is there any coffee?"

It's safest not to respond to my brother. I chant louder. Sara follows Peter down the stairs. "I'll make coffee," she says going to her home, her safe place, the kitchen. "How about some eggs? I have spinach and cheese. I can make an omelet."

"Just do coffee. I've booked a flight out at noon." It's good that Peter will be gone soon.

"How about you, Florence? Want an omelet?" Sara asks.

I silently hold my Poseidon. Peter taps me on the top of my head. I don't move. He gives me a little kick in my right leg, knocking me out of my warrior pose.

"We need to talk with you about the bridge," he demands.

I shove him back. "I told you that story already."

Peter looks at Sara, imploring her to say something. "Go put some pants on," she says. "You can't walk around here in your underwear."

Once he has gone upstairs, Sara sits down next to me. "It's just that we aren't clear on what happened," she says gently. "If three men attacked you, we should call the police. You could have been killed."

"They can't be found. I think they might be invisible," I say knowing that maybe I shouldn't be sharing this magical secret.

"Invisible?" Sara says cautiously.

"To the police," I explain.

"Three tall men wearing hoods might have been seen," Sara says.

"They were trying to stop me." Can I trust Sara to understand?

"From doing what?" Sara asks.

"They were sent to me. They spoke to me. It was the first time I heard them speak."

"You saw these men before that night?" Sara straightens her back as if a chill is moving up her spine.

"I see them. Yes. Sometimes they appear in my pictures," I say, trying to make my words sound causal.

"Why didn't you tell me about this before?"

"You weren't ready to know. They're looking for me. They'll find me again."

"And this doesn't scare you?" Sara starts to put an arm around me but she stops. I think she is afraid that if she touches me, I'll stop talking.

"Not now. I'm powerful. Don't look so frightened. When I came to your house I surrounded it with a shield so that they can't get to us here. We're perfectly safe." I decide that it's safe to let Sara in.

"I'll tell it all to you, so you can know what I know."

"Peter," Sara calls up the stairs. "Get down here. Florence is going to tell us what happened."

"Okay, coming," his voice comes first and then I see him, slipping his precious bottle of Xanax into his pants pocket as he comes downstairs. He sits on the sofa with Sara. "We're listening Florence. Go for it."

"It's not for Peter. Just for you, Sara."

"Please," Sara begs me. "Peter will be nice. We're a family. I want him to know what happened too."

"Will you be nice, Peter?" I ask.

"Of course," he says. I don't trust his words. But I'm ready now and the story is ready too. Peter and Sara look at me like they are in a theater waiting for the show to start. Okay, I will be their show. I stand before them to perform my story.

"I just discovered who I really am," I say slowly, waiting for them to come into the story with me.

"Before or after the bridge?" Peter asks.

"Before, of course. Everything is before."

"It was a month ago I think. I was in bed listening for rain but there wasn't any that night. The sky was perfectly clear, almost as bright as day. I looked out the window and saw a hovering globe of white light. I thought it was an alien thing from outer space."

Peter is looking at his watch. I know what he is thinking. Only three hours and he will be away from me. He wants to take his Xanax. He has no imagination. He thinks my life is a lie, a fantasy.

"So *was* it a space ship?" Peter asks, with a little sarcastic laugh.

I laugh too. "No, of course, not. It was the full moon, so clean and perfect, hanging low in the sky."

I have to start off slowly so he doesn't assume this is going to be a made-up story.

But I'm just getting started.

"During the winter when the sun leaves the sky for the longest time the moon doesn't cross high in the sky as usual, but creeps low near the earth. This special night happens only once a year. It is called the night of the Wolf Moon."

"I've heard of that," Sara says excitedly, looking at Peter. "The Wolf Moon is the first full moon of the new year and the time when it appears lowest in the sky."

"See. This is all real." I am delighted that they're getting it.

"The men who have been sent... the watchers tell me—"

"Wait. The *watchers*?" Peter interrupts.

"Yes, they say that on this night the moon sails so low that it actually touches the earth, and in that second a new Guardian is chosen. Always a young woman who can hold the moon's power.

"When the thin clouds hang like a cotton mist over the grasslands, the chosen one dances across the country, whispering to the people as they sleep. She calls them from their dreams to follow her to a secret place hidden from the sun. Their bodies lie sleeping. She steals only their souls on her midnight haunts. Those who are brave enough follow her to a secret place where the magic begins.

"The owls, the cougars, the horses, the eagles all come to see her. They approach her timidly because they know how powerful she is. Then, just for one night, each person is allowed inside the body of the animal they choose.

"She brings the animals the greatest gift on earth, a human mind. If you are lucky you will race, hunt and kill inside the cougar.

The memory of his attack will live in your mind and you will become a warrior, a soldier, a murderer.

"If you are given the owl, you will remember flight and night vision, and you will learn to see the souls of men. If you are unlucky the snake or the lizard will carry you for the night and your body will remember to eat dust and always to look up to see others.

"At dawn when the moon sets, she calls back the minds of the people she has taken before they wake. But sometimes one of the night creatures is loathe to give up so great a gift and it runs away challenging the sunrise, refusing to give the back the mind. When this empty person wakes, she gives them the soul of someone who has died during the night. She is the keeper of souls."

"Is that a folk story you read or did you make it up?" Sara asks and I'm happy that she looks mesmerized.

"It's not a story, it's true."

"What does it mean?" Sara asks.

"It's who I am."

"Are you one of those people with the stolen mind?" Sara asks.

I laugh. "No, of course not."

"So this is a metaphor for something?" Peter asks.

I have to explain it to Peter. "In every generation one person is selected to carry the lost souls…to guard them until they can be released. I am the one chosen. I am Chandra."

"Now you're freaking me out," Peter says.

"I am the moon."

Chapter 12

PETER

I AM SITTING IN THE EXECUTIVE lounge at the United Airlines VIP terminal. I pop a Xanax with a cup of coffee. It'll take at least twenty minutes to kick in. In five hours I'll be back in New York, just in time to make my weekly poker game. Then this whole thing will be out of my hands.

The morning had rattled me. It was clear that a screw had loosened in Florence's mind. This wasn't just another one of her crazy escapades. This time she might really be crazy. Maybe I should blow off my flight and stay in Seattle at least until somebody figures out what to do about Florence.

My flight has been postponed for over an hour now. The weather is still bad, but I have been assured by the smiling face of the young woman assigned to the gate that planes are taking off and I will get out to New York in the next few hours. My usual fear of flying goes into high gear whenever I have to wait for a flight.

The Xanax might wear off before the flight and I'll have to take another one. The tiny white pills are a miracle of calm. Twenty minutes after swallowing one, I can feel my body melting into a softer, spongier state. The problem is they're addictive. Worse than heroin to get off of, my doctor had said, giving me a prescription for thirty tablets, which at the rate I'm taking them is a two-week supply. So I went to another doctor that one of the guys in the office recommended. "Call the Wall Street Wizard," he said and I did. So I now have a hundred-pill safety net.

Mixing Xanax with a couple of cocktails is probably not the best idea, but neither is shooting through the air in a steel tube over the entire country. Whenever my work forces me to travel along the eastern seaboard I go by train. That comes with its own fears of hurtling at a hundred miles an hour into an inattentive deer or a drunk driver trying to make it through the barrier before it closes. But at least I'm not 30,000 feet up in the air.

Boarding. Finally. What had Florence said about protecting us? Something about putting a shield…protective shield around the house so that no harm could come to us. Not such a bad idea. How comforting that would be if I could believe that by the sheer force of my own will, I could put a shield around the plane, protect it from lightning, turbulence, and basically just crashing. The news had been full of stories about an American Airlines plane that had disappeared off the radar screen somewhere in the middle of the Atlantic. The speculation involved something to do with ice crystals forming on the tail. I'll never fly in the winter again.

Once in the air the pilot announces that there's a strong tailwind so we'll be able to make up almost an hour of our delayed time. Good. That'll put me at JFK in time to catch a cab across town for the poker game.

PATRICK AND DON ARE ALREADY two beers up when I arrive. I get one for myself, relieved to be back home. Another beer and my sister's problems slide from my mind.

"Slow week at the shop," Patrick says. "I've got lots of stuff in the pipeline but it's taking its sweet time to come in. What about you guys?"

"I've got some hot leads from a top dog at Lehman," Don says, "but nothing solid."

They are both hoping that they'll hear me say that it's the same on my end.

"Guess I'm going to win tonight," I say. "Last week I bagged a Chinese investment group to the tune of eighty million." I get the expected noises of respect from Patrick and Don. "The kicker is that they bought it without even glancing at a prospectus. I sold it on flash and dance. My cut on the sell is going to be sweet, but besting you two is even sweeter."

I start counting out the poker chips. Let their tongues hang for a while. I know they're dying to hear the whole story.

"Details," Don says snapping his fingers. "The deal is in the details."

"And I thought it was the devil that was in the details," Patrick laughs. "Come on, Peter. When did you know you had them?"

"Okay," I give them a taste. "Don, when you've got a pair and I'm jacking you up, there's moment just before you match my bet when you adjust your glasses. Nine times out of ten that's your *tell.* I know that you'll follow me wherever I go and that you've got nothing to travel on but a pair."

"I'm going to start wearing my contacts more," Don laughs.

"It's the same thing when I'm putting a deal together," I say. "I could see these guys holding back, afraid of committing. So I hold back too until they're hungry for more data. Finally one of them cracks, and asks a down-the-line question, one that you would only ask if you had already envisioned yourself in a done deal. That's the *tell*. I bring out the candy and they all fall into line."

The rest of the guys arrive with their stories, but still I take the hill.

"The night is yours," Patrick says. "But don't forget I've got India Industrials nibbling at the hook and they might come in even bigger. So the battle to you, but the war, still too close to call."

"Wow," Don whistles. "How long have you been working them?'

"No more shop," I say. "Let's play."

I get the first deal and the right to call the stakes. It never matters what the stakes are. After years of playing together, we have basically all come out about even. I might lose a couple of thousand one week, and the next week make it all back. It doesn't even matter what cards we get. The real pleasure of the game is in bluffing each other. Pushing each other to go a little farther than what we think is a solid bet.

Chapter 13

SARA

I CAN'T BELIEVE THAT PETER is gone. He just upped and left right after that crazy story Florence told us. "You'll figure it out," he said. "You're a teacher, you ought to know how to handle crises. I'll call you when I get to New York." After all the times I've been there for him, he walks out on me now.

The first thing I have to do is get Florence seen by somebody…a doctor who could tell me what is going on. Roger and I had been seeing a family therapist for the year before we split up, but then he had been the one who convinced Roger that the marriage had no future. So cross him off the list. Besides, that therapist is probably dead by now. He looked like he was about ninety-five and that was five years ago. Who else can I call? Can you just pick up the yellow pages to find a psychiatrist? Do I have the right to do this without Florence's permission? What if she refuses to see anyone? After all, Florence didn't think she was sick. After declaring that she was the moon earlier this morning, she ran off to get a cup of coffee at Starbucks.

But if I do nothing, there is always the possibility that Florence will jump off a bridge again and the next time maybe she wouldn't be so lucky.

The next morning I look in on Florence and find her sleeping peacefully. Her mouth hangs open a bit and her breath moves softly in and out of her body. There's no sign of the turmoil that lies within her. I leave a note beside her bed so that she'll know how to contact me at school if she wants to. I have a moment of trepidation about leaving her alone, but I have a job and thirty children who rely on me five days a week. I have a responsibility to be there with them, to bring continuity and learning into their lives. That is what I do, and I do it well.

THE BELL RINGS AND THE children run to their seats. Third graders…they sit waiting for me to begin class. Their faces are still sweet at this age. In two more years they'll walk into their fifth-grade classrooms full of cynical remarks and the beginnings of teenage rebellion. Their teachers will be forced to do more disciplining than teaching. The pleasure that comes from watching a young face light up with the discovery of something new will be lost to peer competitions and boy-girl dramas.

Third grade is my home. The children are still sweet and inno-cent and they love me. Other teachers get cruel nicknames that get whispered in the halls, but not me. Year after year I'm referred to as "cool" Mrs. McClellan. I had planned to change back to my maiden name after the divorce, but I have been called Cool Mrs. McClellan for so long I couldn't bear to see her go.

I still remember my own third-grade teacher, Mrs. Anderson. She'd traveled all over the world and her classroom was full of marvelous things she'd gathered in dozens of different countries. The piano at the back of the room was covered with a lion skin, the head draped over the end, yellow eyes staring at all of us. What a different time that was, just thirty years ago. The principal had asked Mrs. Anderson to remove the lion as it was frightening the children but she strongly refused. She said it was an important part of our education. We needed to know what was out there beyond the narrow walls of our small world. She had a passion for sharing all of her adventures and lighting a fire inside us.

I wonder if she'd be disappointed with me now. I didn't follow in her footsteps, traveling the world, having grand adventures. But then, she did show me what it meant to be a great teacher. I never forgot Mrs. Anderson. I don't want my children to ever forget Cool Mrs. McClellan. I can't share grand worldly adventures with them, but there are still adventures right here all around Seattle that I can make part of their education. I know that if they are having fun on the little field trips I plan, they will be learning more than they can sitting in a room with four walls.

The children's arms are in the air waving the permission slips that their parents have signed so that I can take them on a field trip today. This is a trip that I always do in the winter when it's cold and rainy. I take them underground.

What can be more fun than an underground city? There's one right here in Seattle. It's a network of underground passageways and basements that was ground level when the city was first built in the mid-1800s. It's a great history lesson and a chance for the children to explore a ghost town right under Pioneer Square. I tell them how the city was destroyed by the Great Seattle Fire and instead of rebuilding it as it was before, they built a new city right over the ashes of the old one.

I love to see the excitement in their faces as they look at the old shops and meat markets that are over a hundred years old. One little boy who I am especially fond of, Tommy, runs up to me, puts his arms around my waist and hugs me. "You really are the coolest teacher," he says. "It is so rad down here." I feel his little arms around me and my body aches to hug him back, to kiss his cheeks and tell him how happy his joy makes me. But I hold back, restrain myself from such expressions of physical affection. They're simply not allowed. Last year Jack Larson was let go because he allowed himself to express the affection he had for another third-grade student. It could not have been more innocent.

It's painful to grow so fond of these children who are running all around me in this tunnel of history and not be able to share myself more deeply with them. But we can laugh together and perhaps I can even put my hand on a child's shoulder once in a while or tousle the hair on one of their heads.

Holding them, hugging them, feeling their small bodies next to me is impossible. That's reserved only for parents.

So I am cool Mrs. McClellan, and nobody's mother.

Chapter 14

FLORENCE

I SIT NEXT TO MY SISTER holding her hand in the waiting room of Dr. Richardson's office. I look at the magazines on the table next to the sofa, *Better Homes and Gardens, Vogue, Us.* Who are the people who come to see this man? Why do they want to read these magazines? There's no one else in this tiny room but Sara and me. It's a place designed for waiting, a limbo between the healthy people and the people who have something wrong inside their brains.

A week ago I had laughed Sara off, saying there was nothing wrong with me and I wasn't going to see any goddamn psychiatrist. But I know now that something strange is happening to me.

After Peter left, they came back to me again. I was lying in bed late at night reading when a woman wearing a black cape floated in through the window and sat at the foot of my bed. For the first time since they had arrived in black hoods, I had the eerie sensation that the woman at the foot of my bed was different. That somehow she was a piece of my own mind that had broken off and formed itself into another whole person. Her face was downcast and her eyes were closed. I was afraid to move. I'd never been afraid of them before. This wasn't like all the other times, I thought; maybe this figure is some kind of ghost. Then suddenly the woman's eyes popped open and she stared directly at me.

I screamed.

Sara came running into my room but by the time she got there the woman had disappeared.

I realized I was crying. Sara took me into her arms as she used to when I was a child.

"What's wrong with me, Sara?" I begged her to tell me. "I can't stop them from coming and this time was the worst of all."

"Did someone try to hurt you?" Sara asked.

"No, she didn't move; she just sat there looking at me, and I knew."

"What did you know?"

"She was different from all the rest of them. She knew me. She *was* me!"

Dr. Richardson wants to know why I jumped off the bridge. He wants to know about the hooded figures. He wants to know things that I don't know, that I don't understand. His black turtleneck sweater hugs his lumpy body. He smiles at me like he's the only one that knows anything. But I can see what he's thinking. At the end of the hour he recommends that I spend a few weeks in the psychiatric unit of Seattle Memorial Hospital. Just for observation, he assures me. "That way we can see first hand if something is wrong," he says.

The thought of being locked up in a mental institution terrifies me. I have no intention of letting this man take control of my life when he has only known me for less than an hour. I look to Sara for help.

"What are you observing her for?" Sara asks.

"Well, this might just be an isolated event," he explains. "But we won't know that until we can observe Florence in a controlled setting. Right now we have to assume she's a risk to herself."

"And if it isn't just an isolated event, what is it?" Sara asks.

"Why don't we just wait and see what we learn before we jump to any conclusions?" he says, not looking at me.

"If you were going to jump to a conclusion, what conclusion would you jump to?" I say, forcing him to see me. He turns reluctantly towards me, his small gray eyes evasive and knowing. He turns back to Sara and talks directly to her as if I am not in the room. As if I don't have the capacity to understand what he is saying.

"It's just that we don't like to put a label on these things until we know for sure. A breakdown like this in the middle to late twenties can often mean that the patient is experiencing chemical imbalances in the brain."

"I am not *the patient*. I am this person who is here sitting in front of you and I want to know what you think is wrong with me," I say as calmly as I can.

Dr. Richardson sits in his big comfortable chair trying not to say the terrible word that's been swimming around in my mind for the last week. I'll make him say it. "Schizophrenia. Is that what you are looking for?" I smile at him so that he'll know that I'm not angry or stupid.

"You have to be patient, Florence," he says in a soft condescending voice. "I can't possibly have answers for you today."

Then he stands up and sticks out his skinny, long-fingered hand, offering it to Sara not me. "We have run out of time," he says.

It's your time we have run out of, not mine, I want to yell at him. We've run out of this little piece of your time that you have allotted me before someone else walks through the door. Someone who has been sitting in your tiny waiting room reading boring year-old magazines. Someone who'll get fifty minutes of your precious time before you stand and declare that they too have run out of time. Who made you the *keeper of time*?

But I don't say any of this. I want Dr. Richardson to think that I'm perfectly normal. I don't want him to sign a piece of paper that says I should go to a hospital. But it doesn't matter what I want. Dr. Richardson already has a plan for my life and I have no say in it.

"I'll have my secretary arrange for Florence to check into Seattle Memorial tomorrow morning," he says, shaking Sara's hand and smiling like he has just invited us to take a lovely little vacation.

Then it is over. We leave the office in silence. I don't say a word until we're outside this building of doctors. Once we're safely inside the car and driving away, I look to Sara for help.

"I'm not going to a hospital. They can't make me do that, can they?"

Sara looks frightened. I can see she is trying to decide if the hospital is the right thing to do. Finally she says, "Maybe a second opinion would be a good idea."

"The only opinion that matters is mine. I'm not going to a hospital," I say angrily. If I am strong enough, Sara won't go against my will.

Sara tries to calm me down. "It would just be for a few weeks. That's what the doctor said, wasn't it? Just a few weeks while they give you a medication that will make your delusions go away."

She's on their side now. Delusions, that's their word not mine. And what if I don't want them to go away? What if they care about me more than Dr. Richardson or even Sara?

Sara tries to reason with me. "Listen, Florence, research in the area of mental problems has come a long way. Maybe this isn't going to be that bad. With these drugs, you can probably live a normal life."

"If I go to a hospital, I'll never come out," I scream at her.

OKAY, IF I AM SEEING PEOPLE who aren't really there, then it's my brain that created them. Why can't I uncreate them as well? That makes sense. I'm the one in control. It's my mind.

When the woman in black floats in again tonight and sits at the foot of my bed, I sit up and look directly at her. "You aren't here," I tell her. "You don't exist."

I'm startled when the old woman's face lights up and a soft laugh rolls out of her thin mouth.

"No," I shout. "You don't have power over me. Go away. I decide this. I can't see you."

The woman rises and slowly walks around the bedroom. Then she moves towards the bed.

"Stop. Don't come any closer," I tell her. "It's not like before. I know that you live in a bad part of my brain, not in the real world. I'm telling you to disappear."

She freezes in place.

"Good," I tell her. Then I begin singing softly, so that Sara wouldn't hear me. I sing "Amazing Grace." The woman stands perfectly still while I sing. But the moment the song ends and silence returns she begins to move towards the bed once again.

"*You* can't stop me." The woman speaks, her voice tinny and cold.

I jump out of bed and confront her. "I can. I can!"

The eerie laugh comes again from her mouth. "You're the one

keeping me here. Bringing me back. You're holding my soul so I can't move on."

"I don't want your soul."

"Then let me go."

"I don't know how," I tell her.

"Yes, you do. If you don't exist, I don't exist. It's easy."

"It's not easy," I say.

The woman laughs again. "You don't have the courage. You pick low bridges."

"You wanted me to drown."

"I don't want things. You want them," she says, like she's talking to a child.

"I don't want to die," I protest.

"Maybe. Maybe not."

After three nights of appearances by the old woman at the foot of my bed, I agree to check into the hospital. A team of doctors comes to the conclusion that I probably *am* suffering from schizophrenia and it would be best to start a course of antipsychotic drugs under strict hospital supervision.

No one can ever understand how frightened I am.

SPRING 2008

Chapter 15

PETER

I'T'S THE MIDDLE OF APRIL when I drive up to Connecticut. After weeks of bleak weather, the sun is finally out, giving me a flicker of hope. My trips up to visit Mary Ellen have been less frequent. It's getting harder and harder to leave New York. Everyday is a new crisis. Everyone is tense and waiting for the other shoe to drop after Bear Stearns' collapse in March.

It feels good to be out on the road. I'm looking forward to the open country and Mother's farmhouse.

After a lifetime with a stubborn will and an incredible resilience, I think my mother is starting to lose pieces of her memory. Her body is still in amazing shape but her mind tends to skip beats. The irony is not lost on me: two of my family members at opposite ends of life with strong bodies and fractured brains.

Mary Ellen is balancing precariously on a short ladder in the breakfast room when I arrive. Her overalls are covered in purple paint. The walls are half covered in the same color.

"'Why don't you get a handyman to do that for you?" I offer in greeting.

"Why should I?" she says, not turning around to acknowledge my arrival. "I've already got a handy*woman*, me, and I can do a better job than any of the locals I'd have to pay. If you're so concerned about it, pick up a brush and help me."

I haven't painted anything since I was a kid. I figured this is a task you hire professionals to do. It had cost me a fortune to have my apartment painted, with its sixteen-foot ceilings. But what the hell, if Mary Ellen can do it so can I. I pick up a brush, dip it in the purple paint and spend the next three hours taking instructions from my mother.

"Your job is to clean up the edges for me. Once I get it all rolled on you go back and cut the corners in." She barks orders to me as if I am the volunteer crew assigned to finishing the job. As we work I start talking about what's going on in New York, what's happening on Wall Street, but she interrupts me quickly. "Oh, Peter, don't let's waste our time talking about all that. I know you're a big wheel in the city. That's why you come up here, isn't it? So I can take you down a peg." She gives me a friendly poke me in the ribs with the handle of her brush. "You missed a spot."

When we finish, we step back and admire our work. My mother spent a year in Santa Fe, New Mexico the year before she married my father and moved to New England. The rich colors of the Southwest had bled into her bones and she has decorated every place we lived as if it stood in the middle of the desert. We never had a white wall or even a beige one in our home. She loved primary colors, bright reds, yellows, and blues. And now purple.

"It looks great," I tell her and I mean it. My own walls are boring by comparison.

My approval or disapproval of her purple wall is none of her concern. It was her idea to paint it; she picked out the color; it was her project. It is her achievement and she revels in it.

What a damn elegant woman my mother is, standing straight and proud beside me. Her gray hair hangs to the middle of her back and is still thick and shiny. I once suggested she color it, that she had such a great figure, getting rid of the gray would make her look so much younger.

"Why do I need to look younger?" she laughed. "Do you think that old quarter horse is going to feel better if he thinks he's got a young girl on his back? I liked this hair when I was forty, and I like it fine now. No," she said, "the only thing that gets painted around here is the walls."

We clean up the mess from her painting project and have lunch on the back porch. I'd forgotten that I'd brought her flowers from a little roadside stand on the way up.

She pushes them away when I offer them. "I don't want those," she purses her lips in disapproval. "Throw them away. Why did you go and buy flowers anyway? What a waste." Then she gives me a slow teasing smile, "This is spring, the hills are alive with flowers. We'll ride out this afternoon and pick some of our own."

"You're not getting me back on a horse," I protest.

The word "no" is not in Mary Ellen's lexicon. Once she's set her mind to something it doesn't much matter what I say.

"Henry brought over that little filly you rode last time. She's half the size of my quarter horse so you ought to be able to handle her." She changes into jeans and chaps. Then I see her pulling on her well-worn riding boots.

"I thought you said that the cleaning lady stole your riding boots."

"Turns out she didn't steal them, she was just taking them to be cleaned. That's her job isn't it?" She winks just to be sure I get the joke. "Get ready, we're going riding."

There is no arguing with my mother. She saddles up the two horses and we ride up the hill behind her farmhouse. At first it's a gentle walk but I know from experience that soon we are going to break into an uncomfortable trot that my butt and thighs will feel for the next week. What I don't expect is the moment when Mary Ellen makes a sharp clicking sound, gently pushes her heels into her horse's ribs, and takes off in a gallop. My horse obediently follows. I grab the horn, which I vaguely remember is the last thing you're supposed to do, and pray that I can stay on her back until my mother remembers that her son has no idea how to ride a racing horse and decides to slow down.

I survive the afternoon ride, no thanks to my mother.

Once we are safely back in the barn, I watch her brushing down her own horse, who she named Lady Grace, because she says the big horse still can canter like a blue blood. She hums as she brushes, not a song or a melody, but just a sound like a cat purring. And in this moment I realize I envy her. I envy her serenity. She's so good at living inside her own skin. Then, forgetting that I'm even there, the humming turns into a song.

"I'm coming back someday, come what may, to Blue Bayou," she sings. I feel goose bumps rise to my skin. This is the same reaction I had when I was a child whenever Mary Ellen broke into song. Her voice was so rich and compelling and she sang with such passion and abandon that you couldn't help but be drawn into her world.

When we get back to the house I tell her, "Sara called last night. She thinks that maybe Florence is getting better," I'm lying. Why do I even bother? When I finally told Mary Ellen that her youngest daughter was in a mental hospital, it didn't raise a reaction.

"You do remember Florence, don't you?" I ask her.

"Of course. I'm not around the bend yet."

"Do you want to go out to Seattle with me to see her?"

"Seattle. What are you talking about? My sister Florence died years ago."

This knocks me back. I know she mixes up names and sometimes can't remember even important information about the lives of her three children, but this is over the top. I had joked to Sara just a few months ago that Mary Ellen didn't remember Florence. I didn't know how true this was going to turn out to be.

"No, not that Florence. I'm talking about the daughter that you *named* after your sister. Your twenty-seven-year old daughter who lives in Seattle."

The thing is, my mother was always uninterested in anything that didn't have an immediate effect on her. Maybe it had become worse with age, but it had always been there.

When she gets caught in one of her little confusions, as she calls them, she changes the subject. "Last week I walked over to that old shoe store in the mall and bought these shoes," she says as if she is about to reveal secret information. "That fast-talking salesman told me that they were good for walking. Walking where, I asked him? The soles are stiff as bricks…they're only good for walking up a ladder. But he said they would break in and in just a few weeks I'd be swearing by them saying they were the best shoes I ever owned. He was full of crap. The canvas shoes I got at J.C. Penney three years ago are better. Nine dollars and fifty three cents I paid for those sweet little shoes. Rubber soles, so easy that I never got a pain in my feet. They finally fell apart last month so I went back to get some more and they don't carry them anymore. Nothing is like it used to be."

"That's true, Mom."

"Come into the living room. You can read to me. No one reads to me. We still haven't finished that mystery you brought me a month ago."

Mary Ellen's worsening eyesight was the biggest thing she complained about.

"If your vision is so bad, how can you ride a horse?" I ask

"It's not the horse that's going blind," she laughs. "And he's the only one who really needs to see where he's going. Besides, I can see far away just fine. It's the close-up stuff that gives me problems."

"Your new reading glasses aren't helping?" I ask.

"Honey, they have to make glasses an inch thick for me. The weight of them would topple me over."

I feel sorry for her since I know she fiercely loves her independence and her quiet nights reading novels. At first she had hated the idea of hiring someone to read to her but in the end she had grown fond of the idea of lying comfortably on the sofa and hearing a story read to her.

"I thought we hired Amalia to read to you," I say.

"I had to let her go. Poor thing, everything she read sounded the same. Five minutes of her dreadful monotone voice and I'd be asleep."

"I could find someone else."

"No, that's what I have you for."

Chapter 16

FLORENCE

I T IS NEVER QUIET HERE. People walk the halls all through the night. I hear them opening doors, talking to one another, pushing equipment with metal wheels on hard floors. I've been here for two months. I don't sleep. Maybe for an hour, then someone comes in to check on me, maybe to listen to my heart, to check what these drugs being pumped into me are doing to my mind and to my body. They don't need to bother. I could tell them they've screwed my body up. Made my limbs slow, heavy, stiff, and achy. I have no appetite. I miss the woman in black sitting at the foot of my bed talking with me, I miss Sara, but mostly I miss myself. I wonder if I will ever see me again.

It's April now. When I first came here they said two weeks and she can go home but then they said it wasn't enough, that they needed to up the dose of drugs and wait two more weeks to see what would happen. They waited, I waited, and then it was two more weeks and two more weeks until I lost count.

Doctors and nurses come and go with their cheery false faces, their practiced clichés. "You're looking good. The medications are starting to work. It will be no time before you're able to go home. You've got to stay positive. Think good thoughts. Eat your pudding."

I smile back and make the faces they want me to make so that they'll think I'm getting better and they'll open the doors to this hell hole and let me fly free.

Secretly I want to kill them all. I want to wipe the smiles from their faces and the optimism from their voices and invite them inside my brain. Let them see what they are trying to quiet. Show them all the things that are hiding in the crevices that their powerful drugs will never clean out. Like little sponges, scrubbing mud from the bottoms of corrugated boots, their drugs scrub my brain hoping to wipe it clean to start me anew. Indiscriminately they move around inside my head, under my skull, taking away all that shouldn't be there and all that was once me.

There is a soft knock at the door. I know it's not the nurses coming to drain my blood one more time. They don't knock; they just walk in, click on the bright light, stick needles in my arms and care not at all that it's three in the morning. No, I know this knock; it doesn't belong to the white coats. It is another alien friend who sneaks out of his room every night and comes to sit on the edge of my bed and talk with me.

"Are you awake?" Dennis asks the same thing each night knowing full well that I am…that I always am and that I wait for him and that the night is less black the moment he enters my room.

I whisper, "Yes, I'm awake, yes. Come in quickly." Dennis doesn't turn the lights on. He walks quietly to the foot of my bed and sits, his baggy flannel pajamas spread out covering my feet. Sometimes we just sit like that for a while and don't talk at all. It takes us time to find our words. The drugs have taken away so many of them that our thoughts are silenced. Thoughts bounce against our skulls and we listen to each other inside.

Dennis has been in this psychiatric ward for six months. I want to ask him if he thinks we'll ever get out of here, if there will ever be a time when our brains heal enough for us to walk safely among the regular people. I'm not naïve. I know that there is no cure for schizophrenia and that I will live with this the rest of my life. But I want to hear Dennis tell me that it gets better, that there is a place between feeling numb and feeling too much. I will never ask him these questions because there is only one answer I want to hear and I don't think he can lie to me.

Doctors and nurses give you all the lies you want and I give them right back. "Anything is possible," they say. "It's hard to predict these things. Everyone is different. The medications affect each person differently." There are no straight answers. I am still in the limbo that was Dr. Richardson's waiting room.

The person that came in here two months ago, the person that was me, was much easier to live inside of than the person they have made me now. What good is a hospital that makes you feel worse instead of better? I want to go back to the way I was before.

"You look scared," I tell Dennis. "Did you have another night-mare?" Dennis is like me. He hears voices and sees people that he's told don't exist. But they don't call him schizophrenic. They call it Post-traumatic Stress Disorder. He has a disorder, I have a disease, but we live in the same world and we know each other.

Dennis got back from Iraq a year ago. He can't remember how many people he killed, but when he is awake enough he will tell me some of the stories. He dreams about them, the dead people, every night and he says those dreams are worse than the ones when others are trying to kill *him*, worse than the night he stepped too close to an IED and his world exploded. His clearest memory of that night is not his own pain as bits of steel, gravel and stone pierced his skin and bones. It is the face of a young Iraqi mother holding her baby and then crumbling into pieces before his eyes.

I tell Dennis every night that the dreams will go way, that they will not haunt him for the rest of his life. He knows I'm lying. He knows because we are the same. He tells me that long before he went to Iraq, he heard voices like I did. He knew the word *schizophrenia* long before he put on a uniform and shipped off to a hell that he thought might be less frightening than the hell inside his own mind.

Sometimes we talk about little things, what we like to eat, what we can still taste.

Tonight I need for him to help me understand.

"I knew I was doing risky things," I tell him, "but it never occurred to me that all of my behaviors over the last five years could be coming from inside my head. There was always some reason that I could find for my actions, some explanation that didn't involve neurons misfiring and sending me false messages."

"It was the same for me," he says. "They just put me on a new antipsychotic drug. It's one of those things that is all consonants, probably comes from the Greek. Zyprexa. It would make a great word for Scrabble wouldn't it? A Z and an X and even a Y. It must be about a thousand points."

"They keep changing my drugs," I tell him. "They started me on Haldol and then decided it wasn't going to work on my symptoms. I have no clue how they decided that. They don't even know what my symptoms are."

"Do they?"

"What do you mean?"

"Florence, are you lying to your therapist?" he teases me.

"Not lying," I say. "I'm just not sure they need to know every-thing I know. Come on, Dennis, I'll bet you lie to your therapist too."

"Of course," he says. "And I'm getting really good at it. I tell her just what she wants to hear: all the terrible war stories. On some level I think I'm her entertainment, her movie of the week."

After a while he lies down in the single bed with me and we put our faces close together. We talk about going home even though neither one of us has a real home to go to. We talk about our fami-lies. I can even get him to laugh sometimes when I tell him stories about Peter, how I loved to screw with him when I lived with him in New York. When he stops laughing though, Dennis speaks the truth that I am willing to hear only from him. He says I did all that stuff to try and get Peter's attention, to get him to notice me, see me, care about me.

I want to ask Dennis if he thinks we'll ever get out of here.

Sometimes Dennis takes my hand and we cry a little together.

That is the happiest part of my day.

Chapter 17

PETER

P LEASE, PLEASE COME OUT," Sara's phone messages are now more urgent. "Florence is getting worse all the time. It's like her personality is disappearing. They keep telling me that it's just a reaction to the medications and once her body gets used to them she won't be so tired. This can't be right, Peter. I would rather see her crazy, even jumping off bridges than slowly turning into somebody who isn't really there. I don't care how much you hate flying. Get on a train, for Christ's sake; you can be here in two days."

I'll go, I promise myself. I will do whatever it takes…whatever drugs it takes to get myself back on a plane and out to Seattle just as soon as things calm down in New York.

The hope that spring would make things better is rapidly falling away. I feel like I'm treading water on all fronts. Things at Lambert & Hall are getting out of hand fast. The hedge fund that had been such an easy sell for so many years is now looking like a sinkhole. Almost all of the securities it contains are leveraged investments in mortgage-backed securities and the sub-prime meltdown is going to bite the whole package in the ass. The floor traders paste on cavalier faces and act as if this is all going to right itself before the summer is out. Secretly I suspect they all know better. You would have to be an idiot to not be scared out of your wits.

The night I arrived home from Mary Ellen's in Connecticut I stayed up all night reading the volumes of information on the securities I sell every day. Why had I never bothered to look at this stuff before? But then nobody did. Nobody knew what they were selling. As I pored over these portfolios I realized there was no way out. It was only a matter of time before someone figured out that the funds weren't worth the paper they were printed on. I logged onto my own trading accounts and began to sell my private securities. At least I could get my own money out before it was gone.

But the next day the Dow was up over a hundred points. I never should have panicked. The Bear Stearns debacle had just scared people. And the sub-prime situation wasn't as bad as I thought it was. That night I bought back a few of the securities I had sold. I had to relax, I told myself. This was America; a bank or two could go down but the economy was still strong. My colleagues were right. It might take a few months, but things would be back to normal by the end of summer.

My optimism faded over the next week when every day I received calls from my clients. They were worried. They were scared. They weren't as naïve and passive as I had hoped they would be. They read the same papers I did. Listened to the same news. They were starting to ask questions about how safe their investments were. If a huge lender like Countrywide could go bankrupt and now Bear Stearns, who was next?

I don't have any good answers. Be calm I would tell them. This will all straighten itself out.

My early-morning runs in Central Park are getting longer

and longer, any excuse for not going into the office, not facing the mounting questions. The talk in restaurants and bars at night focuses only on this economic mess we're all in. Speculating about what might happen becomes the only topic of conversation. At one point in my career I enjoyed all this, the tension and excitement, the adrenaline rush. But now I find myself staying home alone at night, avoiding my friends and the endless circular conversations.

God, how I miss Lydia. Just ending the day with her in my arms, falling asleep with her warm body lying next to me.

Why had she left? It all was a blur. Maybe that was the problem. She wanted to be the center of my focus and I put her in the background behind my work. Now she was gone. Married to what... probably a farmer in the Midwest. A solid guy who thought she was more important than his career.

I need a break. I need to get out of New York. But the last place I want to go is Seattle.

"They're releasing her from the hospital next week," Sara's message said. "She'll be staying with me. And by the way, I've been sort of laid off. In a month school will be out and the summer sessions I would have taught have been canceled because of budget cuts. So, my dear brother, your sister is unemployed and without prospects. At least for the summer. I don't know if I'll have a job in the fall or not."

This time I call her back immediately. This is a concrete problem that I can do something about. I have no idea how to help Florence but if Sara has a problem that I can solve by throwing money at it, I'm happy to do so.

"What do you need? I can lend you money. That's no problem."

"I don't need money, at least not yet. What I need is you here. I need family and unfortunately, you're all I've got."

"You have no idea what's going on here," I say. "Have you even read a newspaper in the last few days? The whole of Wall Street is frantic."

"I read," she says, with an uncharacteristic edge to her voice.

"God, how did my life get so fucked up?" I say.

"You make it sound like it's all happening to you. Do you think this is the life that Florence would have picked?"

I soften my tone. "How can you handle all this?"

"What choice do I have?"

"Don't go there with me, Sara. You have choices. Don't play the victim."

"Peter, you don't understand, she's got no one but us. It's our obligation to take care of her"

I listen but I'm safely three thousand miles away. I'm here for advice but the heavy lifting will all fall on Sara's shoulders.

"I'll come out soon," I say without conviction.

"She asks about you," Sara tosses out.

"Why don't I believe that?" I say.

"It's true. The first few weeks in the hospital she kept asking for both of us. Well, sort of. It was more like 'Where are my people?' That's us, Peter."

"It's more likely she's asking for her *invisible* people. The ones that told her to jump off a bridge."

There's a silence at the other end of the phone.

"Maybe," Sara's voice deflates. "I didn't think of it that way."

Sara never sticks to her guns. I can get her to change her mind on a dime. With just one sentence I can turn her around and get her to see things from my point of view. Changing peoples' minds quickly is one of the basic skills required to be a top-notch fund salesman. Maybe not the best idea to use it on my sister. But Christ, she's got to learn to stand up for what she believes.

Sometimes I just want to yell at her, "Get a spine, Sara."

Chapter 18

FLORENCE

THE WINDOWS DON'T OPEN. All doors and windows in the psych ward are locked shut to keep us in and the real world out. I want to feel the cold night air, breathe in the dampness, the wind. Not this carefully measured hospital air that smells like rubbing alcohol and stale heat.

I can see a sliver of a moon through the glass. She still calls to me. I don't know if I'll ever be able to walk with her again.

I remember once when I was a child, not more than five years old, when the moon came to life. It was 3 A.M. on a hot summer night. I remember the heat baking my small third-floor bedroom. I went to the window to let in the night air. And just as I pulled aside the yellow curtains I saw a slight movement, a shadow that caught the corner of my eye. The full moon held me mesmerized. I waited to see if the shadow would return, and it did. A figure leading one of the mares from the barn. It crossed into the light of the moon until they were one, the woman and the moon walking together. The woman with red hair, loose and wild, hanging below her waist. In a single swift move the woman jumped on the back of the mare. Holding her mane, she touched the mare's flanks with her bare heels and they galloped off straight into the moon.

That's how I remember it now.

The woman was my mother. How spectacular she was to me, with her long red mane flying in the night.

I NEED TO FEEL SOMETHING that is real again. To wake me up, wake up my body. When Dennis kissed me last night, his tongue rolling around mine, we both stopped at the same time. We pulled our lips apart and stared at one another with disappointment.

"I want to turn you on," he said.

I understood him. He didn't mean sexually. I was dark inside and he wanted to click the switch that would turn on the lights again, the lights the drugs had turned off. I wanted to do the same for him. We lay in my bed in each other's arms but there was a well of numbness between us like cobwebs around our brains. We felt the need for each other, without the ability to do anything about it.

He'll be back tonight. If only I could open a window for him. Give him some air.

They say I can go home next week, that I'm no longer a danger to myself. What do they know? I used to feel like I was a danger to *them*. Given the opportunity and the right tools, there are at least two doctors and four nurses I would have liked to push off a bridge. I remember the pleasure of feeling that anger. It was juicy and crisp. It tasted like onions in my mouth. I liked that my emotions have developed taste. I wanted to know what frustration, sadness, happiness, all of them tasted like. All I could taste was the onions. And even that is gone now. All my feelings are quiet, just like they wanted me, quiet, no voices, no visions.

They don't promise me that they won't come back again, the delusions. They can break through, they explain, and I am to understand that they aren't real and the best thing I can do is distract myself and ignore them. Basically, they say, I can go back to my normal life, which is impossible since I have no idea what that is.

Dennis doesn't knock anymore. He just appears in my bed at three in the morning.

"They're letting me out tomorrow," he tells me.

"I'm out next week," I tell him. "So is this all over? Will we see each other?"

"Of course, you're my girl. We're going to help each other make it back."

"Is that possible?" I say, knowing how good we are at lying to one another.

"Sure, you're strong. You're going to beat this back. Find a balance between the drugs and your own spirit." He holds me and we are quiet for a long time. I'm afraid the night nurse will find us.

"Florence, you know that you have kept me alive in here."

"The same for you," I say, wishing we could make love, that I could give myself to him. I know he wants to, but his body doesn't respond.

"I'm sorry," he says.

He says these words so sadly. I don't know what he means he's sorry for. Maybe just for all of it, for us both living in the clouds and fog, or maybe he means something more specific.

After about an hour he crawls out of my bed thinking I am asleep. I feel his body pull away from mine. I feel the bed lighten without his weight. I hear his bare feet touch the cold floor and then the heavy hospital door close behind him.

*****

Voices, loud, calling frantic commands to one another wake me the next morning. I hear people running down the hall outside my room. I hear carts being wheeled, male voices shouting to female voices.

I get out of bed, moving slowly. There is a strange cold fear running through my body. I want to run out into the hall to see what is happening, but my legs won't move quickly in the morning. They seem to wait for my mind to wake them, to give them the commands that they require in order to move.

I make it to the door to my room. I hesitate. Something bad is waiting on the other side. If I open this door, that badness will come inside me and take up residence in my body. I turn the handle and open the door a crack, just enough to look down the hall and see that all the attention is being focused on Dennis's room, four doors down from mine. Finally some adrenaline wakes up my limbs and pushes me down the hall. Not Dennis, I think, please, let nothing have happened to Dennis.

Nurses see me and try to push me back to my room. I ignore them. For just this one minute my will is stronger then theirs. I get to the door of Dennis's room. There are doctors and nurses all around him and blood, blood everywhere, blood covering the floor.

I hear one of the nurses say it must have been the electrician who was here last night fixing the switches. And then another voice, who would have thought you could do this with a screwdriver.

This isn't possible I tell myself. He was lying with me just a few hours ago promising that we would make it back together. He must have known then that he was going to do this. I can't comprehend what is happening. I know this isn't a dream or a delusion, that it is real and it is done and it is forever and it will change everything.

I see one of the white coats stand above Dennis. I hear him say, let's call it 6:13 AM. All the air is sucked from the room. I can't breathe. I run back through the hallway of nurses and doctors, back to my room. In the closet are the clothes I had when I checked in. Jeans and a sweatshirt, my gym shoes. I dress quickly, go back out into the hall.

They are all so busy that they don't notice me as I run past the elevators to the stairwell. I take the steps two at a time. I haven't moved this fast in two months. When I get downstairs to the psych ward entrance that is always locked I see more technicians arriving with medical equipment.

They don't know yet that they are too late, too late for Dennis but not too late for me. When they come through the door in a hurry I slip past them out the front door of the hospital. The cold air feels wet against my face. I don't know why, since it isn't raining. Then I realize that I am creating the wet myself. I haven't cried in so long. You have to be able to feel to cry. Maybe I'm not completely gone, maybe I can run away from all of this. Wake up in a park somewhere and discover that none of it has been true. I am my old self again.

It's a lie, it's all a lie there is no me and Dennis is gone.

There is nothing to do but run.

Chapter 19

SARA

THE SUN IS PEEKING through the clouds. This is the first morning in three weeks that I don't wake up to the sound of rain. And this happens on a Saturday. No teaching job to go to and a whole day in front of me. I have been going to see Florence on Saturdays but I'll see her tomorrow. I need to do something that is just for me today. Another teacher has been telling me about a day spa that she goes to and how relaxing it is, like a vacation packed into a few hours.

I look through the Yellow Pages and find the place she has been talking about, the Golden Gardens day spa. They have a cancellation; they can get me in for a massage this morning. With every massage you get the use all the other amenities at the facility, the hot tub, the sauna. It sounds perfect. I don't think I've had a massage since Roger and I went to Palm Springs for our second anniversary. He played golf all day and sat in the bar at night while I swam in a pool heated to 85° then had massages and manicures. It was lovely, all that pampering. That trip should have been my first clue that our marriage was on the way out. We both had a great five days mostly because we hardly saw one another. Two months later we were in divorce court.

God I can't believe that was five years ago. Five years since I've had a massage. Five years since I've had a man! How did I let this happen to me? I guess that kind of long-term celibacy sneaks up on you. Weeks become months, months become years and you just forget that sex used to be an important part of your life. What I miss most isn't the actual sex but the intimacy, lying in bed with a man with his arms around me. Someone to touch me.

So maybe having a massage is paying someone to touch me. I want that. I want to feel someone's hands moving along my back, my spine. Rubbing my toes, massaging the back of my neck. The more I think about it the more excited I get. Why have I waited so long to do this? I grab my purse and am half-way out the door when the phone rings.

It's the hospital. The nurse at the other end of the line is both apologetic and frantic. I try to get her to slow down so I can understand what she's saying. She tells me that there's been a terrible tragedy in the psych ward that morning, that a boy committed suicide by pulling the veins from his wrist with a screwdriver. I find myself wondering why I need to know the details of his death. What has this got to do with me? What has this got to do with Florence?

In all the confusion of the morning, the voice on the phone tells me, Florence must have slipped out of the hospital. Slipped, I say, thinking that is something you do before you fall, slip on a stone or a rock. "But isn't it a locked facility?" I say, not understanding what she's telling me. Well, she says, there were so many people coming and going I think Florence may have managed to get through our security. She wasn't in her room when her breakfast was brought, so the whole facility was searched and she couldn't be found.

"Where is she," I ask. "Where could she go?"

"We really have no idea that's why we wanted to inform you right away as you are her contact person. I suggest you find her as soon as possible. We think she may have witnessed the suicide. The boy, his name was Dennis, was a friend of hers. They spent a good deal of time together during the day and we have reason to believe that he visited her room at night. She may be in shock, so locating her quickly is of the utmost importance."

Locating Florence. How am I going to do that? She had come back into my life with so little baggage, so little background information. I didn't know who her friends were, where she hung out. Her friend Dennis had killed himself and I didn't even know who Dennis was. In the whole time she'd been in the hospital I had never met him. Did she see him die in that terrible grotesque way? God, I have to find her. The only phone number I have is that of her old roommate. I drop my bag and coat and look for my address book, thankful that I'm so organized. I find the number immediately and dial it.

The phone is picked up on the second ring. I quickly explain to Betsy, Florence's former roommate, who I am and what I'm trying to do. Has she any idea where Florence might be? Betsy hasn't got a clue where Florence is or where she might go. She hasn't seen Florence since she moved out in January. She does mention the yoga studio but I already have that number and plan to call it next. I implore her, if Florence calls or comes over to please call me immediately. She agrees but there is a tone of indifference in her voice and I can tell that whatever predicament Florence is in, Betsy doesn't want it to be any concern of hers.

My next call is to the yoga studio with pretty much the same results. Florence hasn't been to a class since early February. I start to panic. How do I start looking for her? I can't just drive around Seattle and hope to find her. Where would she go? I have to do something so I grab my purse and coat and go out to the car. I drive aimlessly around the neighborhood to see if she might be coming back to my house. I have to be calm and think this through; if she walked out of the hospital with just the clothes on her back, she doesn't have any money or a way to get around. The hospital is near the city center and I live in West Seattle over the bridge. She could hitch a ride, but she could never get here on foot. Where else could she go? She must feel so frightened and alone. I can't get the image of that boy out of my mind. Driving around isn't going to do any good. I turn around and go back home.

I sit in the living room on the sofa and I can't think of a soul to call. Peter can't help; he's three thousand miles away and would have no idea how to find Florence. I don't have any other phone numbers of her friends. She could just disappear in this city and I could never find her.

What I need is a clue. Suddenly I remember all the photographs she took. She threw hers out before she moved in with me, but I still have some that she gave me before all this happened. I run upstairs to the den and go directly to where I have filed the photographs. There are pictures of people in coats and scarves, bent over, combing the beaches at low tide looking for sea glass. I recognize the beach at Discovery Park. I remember Florence liked to wade out into the ice-cold waters of Puget Sound and shoot back towards the shore to catch these people combing through the piles of driftwood, sea debris, and rocks. I want to jump in the car and drive directly to Discovery Park. Maybe she's there; it's a cold sunny day; she could be looking out at the city walking on the beach. I look through other photos that might be able to identify her whereabouts. Her photography was a sort of meditation for her, a safe place. But which of these safe places might she have gone to today? I take the photos with me and run back downstairs and get back in the car. Sitting in the living room doing nothing is not an option. At least I can try to go to the places where she took what she called sacred pictures. First I drive to Discovery Park. It is an enormous place with miles of trails through beautiful forest trees. White trillium is just beginning to bloom, and the tiny fawn lilies are peeking through the cold ground. The trail I take opens to the empty expanse of the bluffs overlooking the Sound. The wind blows through my coat. I find the path that goes down to the small beach below the bluffs and find it empty. The tide is out but there is no one walking the rocky shore.

It takes me half an hour to get back to my car. There are at least ten more places where I could look for Florence, but at this rate I may not find her before dark. I know in my heart that she's not looking for a friend or shelter. She is looking for a quiet place to be alone.

I pull out a photograph that I recognize as Pioneer Square, near downtown. This would be walking distance from the hospital. It's a place where homeless people come to sit during the day. Florence's photos show these figures slumped over sleeping on benches with newspapers covering their bodies to protect them from the cold. Suddenly I feel hopeful: this makes sense, this is a place where she might go.

I park the car a block from Pioneer Square and walk to what is the oldest part of the city. This is a place I rarely come to, even though it is less than a half a mile from Pike Place Market with all the wonderful shops and restaurants that the tourists love. The

Square looks just like Florence's photos. I see the homeless people who are the subjects of her photos, and then I am shocked and relieved to see her. I guessed right...she is here in Pioneer Square sitting on a bench hunched over next to a man who has clearly passed out beside her.

If I go right up and surprise her she might run away. If I let her see me from a distance first, she still could run away. I walk slowly to her. At first she doesn't see me. When I get ten feet from her I stop. She raises her eyes and looks straight at me. Neither one of us moves for what seems like a very long time. Then I walk to her and sit down beside her. Very slowly I put my arm around her shoulder. Her head falls against my chest and I feel her quietly crying.

She doesn't say anything and neither do I. We stay like that together for a while and then I walk her back to the car. I think about taking her back to the hospital, but that feels wrong. In this moment she trusts me. I open the car door and she gets in and we drive home in silence.

I have no idea what will happen next.

I feel strangely happy as we cross the bridge into West Seattle. I am so proud of myself. I found her and she is safe with me.

Chapter 20

PETER

M Y PLANE WAS SITTING on the tarmac for two hours before it was hauled back to the gate to fix something that was broken. Like an engine. The pilot is making announcements every fifteen minutes reassuring us that everything is under control. They are going to get cleared for take off shortly.

I'm pretty close to a full-blown anxiety attack. There is no way the flight crew is going to let me get off the plane unless it is a life-threatening emergency. Once the aircraft has left the gate, it is considered a departed flight. From that point on, security demands that no one leave the aircraft even if it means keeping hundreds of passengers trapped for hours. If they would let me, I would be off this plane right now, call Sara and tell her I just can't get on another plane. I'm not coming.

Finally we are airborne. I sit in a window seat watching the ground fall away beneath me. I'm nauseated. Sweat beads up on my forehand. I had taken Xanax an hour before the flight was scheduled to take off and I'm worried it will wear off before we even hit cruising altitude. I try taking deep breaths but they only make me feel as if I'm going to hyperventilate.

Closing my eyes I try Florence's technique. I imagine that by the sheer force of my own will I can circle the plane with a protective shield and keep it flying in a weightless bubble, floating safely in the sky. God, maybe I'm as crazy as Florence. Do I really think that my own will and worry could hold up an airplane? Of course this is irrational, but I still feel compelled to do it.

Maybe Sara is the only sane one in the family. Mary Ellen is trotting on her aging horse across Connecticut fields one day and forgetting that she has children the next. Florence has lost reality altogether, and I am treating anxiety with my own delusions.

Then there was the family history to consider. Mary Ellen's younger sister, the first Florence, was also rumored to have been a little batty. She had died under suspicious circumstances in her mid-twenties long before I was born. The official record claimed it was a single car accident, but Mary Ellen had implied over the years that it hadn't been an accident at all. Slamming into a tree at sixty miles an hour was an intentional act. This line of thinking wasn't helping my anxiety. If the original Florence had actually killed herself, then maybe her namesake, my youngest sister, would follow in her footsteps.

An hour into the flight I finally begin to relax. I pull out my laptop hoping I can distract myself and get some work done. In the seat next to me, a plump woman of about eighty pulls out her knitting at the same time and begin softly humming to herself. She wears a hand knitted gray wool sweater even though the plane is hot and stuffy. Her hands, puffy with age, look strangely childlike. Swelling has stretched the skin causing the wrinkles of age to disappear. I watch these hands, amazingly dexterous, move the knitting needles.

Mary Ellen's hands are sharp, angular and bony like the rest of her body. Her whole life she had prided herself on being thin. The rare times when she had allowed me to hug her I can remember only bones pressing through flesh. I have an overwhelming desire to hug the plumpness of the woman sitting next to me, to feel her fleshy arms around my thin body, to have her chubby hands hold my face.

Two hours later, at exactly 10:02, the captain's voice comes on once again. I look at my watch to note the time. It seems somehow important to know the precise time of his words.

"This is your captain. As some of you may have noticed"— what, I think, I didn't notice anything —"we have been losing altitude for the past ten minutes. There is nothing to be alarmed about. We've lost power in our number two engine. This is a Boeing 747, a four-engine aircraft, so we are in no danger. We are designed to fly just fine on three engines. Please relax. The flight attendants will be around shortly with complimentary sodas and wine. Our estimated time of arrival in Seattle is now 12:13 P.M."

My palms go ice cold.

"Don't worry," the old woman smiles at me as if she can read my thoughts. "This probably happens all the time." She doesn't miss a stitch on her knitting.

"Well, it's a first for me," I reply, trying to sound casual. When the flight attendant makes it to my seat I order a Scotch and am surprised when the old woman laughs. "That sounds like a good idea," she says. "I'll have one too."

I find myself laughing with her. And the sound of my own laughter is wonderful.

"It doesn't pay to worry," she says. "It's not in our hands. My name is Esther. I'm going to see my grandchildren."

Grandchildren, I think. There aren't going to be any in our family. We three siblings will have no offspring to carry on the family name. Maybe that isn't a bad thing. Maybe we are just one of those families that are meant to die off, an evolutionary process, weeding out the weak genes.

When our drinks arrive I close my laptop and we two seat mates sip our Scotch together. Normally I would have cut off any conversation having to do with children or grandchildren. I just am not that interested in other people's lives, especially strangers'. But now I want Esther to keep talking and to keep the three-engine aircraft aloft.

Just as I am beginning to feel the effects of the drink, the plane takes a heavy bounce then drops like an unleashed elevator. It stops as suddenly as it started.

The intercom pops on once again.

"This is the captain again. We're trying to fly around a pretty severe thunderstorm over the Rockies. Please put your seats in an upright position and be sure your seat belt is tightly fastened. We're going to hit some bumps."

The nervous voices of almost three hundred strangers talking all at once turns into a din of soft panic and intimate disclosure. I can feel the collective nerves firing throughout the plane.

There is so much I want yet to do with my life. The minute that thought enters my head, it is followed by confusion. Probably everybody feels like this if they think their life might suddenly end. But what is it that I want to do with my life? What was left for me to do?

Esther seems to sense what I'm thinking. She reaches over and takes my hand as the turbulence rocks us. For a half hour we stay like that, our hands clasped, talking of little things. Then I see a bolt of lightning cut through the sky beneath us.

"Aren't you afraid?" I ask the old woman. "We could crash."

The sweet sound of her laughter fills the plane. "You're too dramatic, my dear boy," she says.

"You aren't afraid of death?" I ask, as if posing this question to a perfect stranger is the most natural thing in the world.

She laughs again. "When you've lived as long as I have, you know that death touches every one many times in their lives. You go to the store to buy food and the next day a robber shoots a customer in that store. Death walks with us all the time. You can't make him go away but you can ignore him."

"How do I do that?" I ask like a child wanting to know how to make his toy truck go. "Sometimes I feel afraid of everything."

"Yes," she says. "You look afraid. Perhaps you aren't trying to *ignore* Death. You are just trying to bore him by giving him no opportunities to touch you. You can't be afraid to fly, to live. You think that Death will go away because he is bored because you take no chances. Never. Death has the patience of Job and much more time than we do.

"Look at me," she says with a proud grin. "I have ignored him for eighty-seven years and you can be sure that when I do see him, he won't be bored with the story of *my* life. I have traveled all over the world and had many adventures. My dear boy, give him a good long story and don't let him be bored."

I wonder how life would have been different if this woman had been my mother.

Chapter 21

SARA

I T IS POURING AGAIN. Peter's plane is late. I wait for him in my car outside the terminal. He arrives in a surprisingly good mood. It must've been a smooth, uneventful flight. He doesn't even comment on the weather.

"How is she doing?" he asks without a trace of indifference.

"One step forward, two steps back. The medication is working I guess. She still has delusions sometimes. The doctors say that's to be expected."

"Does that mean she's not bouncing off the walls any more?" he asks.

"She never calls herself Chandra any more. That's a good sign," I say, wanting Peter to see the positive side. "But I hear her sometimes. Talking to herself."

"You mean talking to people who aren't there," he corrects me.

"It's eerie...like the homeless people on street corners talking into the air."

"That's where the schizophrenic population is," he says, "out on the streets."

"Only if they haven't got family," I say, but I can't help imagining Florence sitting alone on a bench in Pioneer Square talking to the air.

As we drive home, Peter tells me about his last visit with our mother. "She dragged me out riding again. God, that woman has more energy than me. She and that old quarter horse are a hell of a team. Horses are the only animals that ever got her respect. Remember when we were kids and I wanted a dog so desperately and Mother wouldn't let us get one?"

I picture Mary Ellen in her red velvet pantsuit appalled at Peter's suggestion that we get a pet. "If it had been up to Dad, we would've had a house full of dogs and cats," I say. "But then nothing was ever *up to Dad*."

Peter imitates Mother, "Fleas and hair all over the house, don't be ridiculous. I'll get you a turtle if you must have a pet." We both laugh. "I thought when I got my own place I would never be without a dog," Peter says. "Flash-forward and no dog ever. I never got one because it was too much responsibility. It would be a burden tying me down. I couldn't travel...just get up and do whatever I wanted."

"You hate to travel," I point out. "Before this, you never left New York unless it was for business."

"I don't mean actually travel. It's just a metaphor for freedom."

"It's good to have something to take care of, even a dog."

"So now you've got Florence to take care of," Peter says. "Be careful you don't end up needing her more than she needs you."

"It's not going to happen," I say without conviction.

*****

When we get home, Peter goes directly upstairs to put his things in his room. He doesn't come down for over an hour. I assume he's on his laptop working. I make some coffee and heat up a berry pie I made this morning. I know that'll get his attention. The aroma will seep into the living room and then up the stairs.

It works. He's down the stairs and into the kitchen, looking for a plate before I can even get the pie out of the oven. I cut us both slices and take them to the coffee table.

"A weird thing happened to me on the plane," Peter says. "There was this old woman—"

"Stop right there. If you describe the same old woman that Florence sees, I'm going to have to check into a psycho ward myself," I say.

Peter laughs. "No, this old gal was flesh and bone and a lot of both. She said some pretty amazing things to me."

"I thought you worked for five hours on a plane and never let anyone talk to you."

"That was the plan. Then an engine gave out…I don't know… I'm thinking that I'm over forty and I'm still waiting for my life to begin…for all the pieces to get in place so I can start living the life I'm supposed to live. It never happens…that one day…that one perfect point when I can start my life the right way."

"I think that's what Florence was trying to photograph before the bridge happened. What did she say? The point when everything is still…no past, no future…a clean point where you can begin."

"No physics to back that up," Peter says. "We all have a boiling point but no still point."

"Taking pictures was her special talent. Your sister has a great eye," I remind him.

"I know. That's why I got her this." Peter pulls a Nikon out of a bag he's left by the door and hands it to me. "She may not even want it."

"It only matters that you bought it for her."

"So what happens now?" he asks, and I know what he means: will she get better?

"I think I've read every book written about it. There's so much stuff to learn. It's a terrible disease. I can't image not knowing what is real and what isn't."

"Maybe in the blur between those two is where all new ideas are born," Peter suggests. "Maybe schizophrenia is nature's way of pushing the brain to change. There must be some evolutionary purpose for it or it wouldn't keep showing up in every generation. Then it could just be chemical accidents, genetic fuck-ups like albino babies. Nature's little mistakes."

"I just don't know how your mind can make you see things that aren't real," I say. "It's too strange a concept to understand. A damaged part of the brain can conjure up not only voices but full three-dimensional visions!"

"Mental holograms," he says, clearly fascinated by the image. "It makes you question everything."

"What do you mean?"

"Well, all the saints had visions. Was Joan of Arc hearing the words of God or was she just schizophrenic?"

"You go in that direction and you end up with all religious beliefs coming from someone's crazy hallucinations," I say, wanting him to get back to Florence.

"It's confusing," he says. "I've been reading this book, *Lying Awake*, about a nun who told her sisters of wonderful conversations she had with God. The convent thought she had a special gift. It turns out she had a brain tumor that was exciting the auditory part of her brain. Doctors wanted to operate and remove the tumor or she would die. She didn't want it removed. She didn't want to lose her connection to God."

"But when she found out it was a tumor, that should have convinced her that it was all in her head," I argue.

"No, you see that's the thing of it. She believed that God put the tumor in her head on purpose so that he could talk to her!"

"Wow. At least Florence isn't that crazy," I say. "She knows on some level that what she sees and hears isn't real. She's really very lucky. This is a very mild form of schizophrenia."

"It's hard to hear *mild* and *schizophrenia* in the same sentence."

"What the doctor said is that there are levels of the disease," I explain. "Florence is what they refer to as high functioning. With drugs and time she could do pretty well."

"But no cure," he says simply.

"No," I admit. "She didn't talk much in the beginning. Now she talks to me. Most of it makes sense. "

"Can her life ever be normal again?" he asks.

"I don't know," I say. "Whose life is normal?"

Chapter 22

FLORENCE

I CAREFULLY CLIMB DOWN the stairs watching each step so that I won't trip and fall. I've slept most of the day and into the night. It's nine o'clock when Sara calls me to come downstairs.

"Hi," I say to Peter. He looks at me, then quickly drops his gaze down so he won't have to stare directly at me. I don't understand until I remember that I've changed since he last saw me. I know there are dark circles under my eyes bleeding into lines that don't belong on my young face. I haven't brushed my hair in days because I like the feel of twisting my fingers through the long strands. I've gotten so thin that this old grey sweat suit hangs on me.

I see Peter catch his breath before he looks in my eyes and forces a smile.

"Good to see you, you're looking much better," he lies.

"I look like shit," I say. "You can say it like it is."

"I'll wash your hair later," Sara says. "That'll feel good." Her voice is full of the artificial air of optimism that I have come to despise.

"Nothing feels," I say, collapsing on the sofa.

"Have you started to do yoga again?" Sara pushes. "That always made you feel better."

"This makes me feel better," I say. "Not moving. I want to

be still."

"Do you feel still now?" Peter asks. This isn't a safe question.

"I told you. Nothing feels." I go into the kitchen to get a glass of water.

Peter whispers to Sara. They talk about me, as if between them they can solve the problem that is me.

"I can hear you," I yell from the kitchen.

"Do you know what we're saying?" Peter asks.

"Yes, I'm crazy, not deaf. You don't have to whisper."

Peter is determined to make this work. "I'm going to be here all weekend. We can do anything you like."

"I can't remember what I like," I say, looking through the freezer. It's full of the ice cream Sara has stuffed in there. She keeps buying different flavors hoping she'll find one that I like. They all taste like cold fat to me. I find the package of frozen peas I'm looking for.

"Can I get you something to eat?" Sara has followed me into the kitchen ready to spring into action.

"Not hungry," I say, taking the peas back to the sofa. It feels good to put them on the back of my neck.

"Well, I'm hungry," Peter says. "I haven't eaten since early this morning. They don't serve meals on cross-country flights any more. Let's order a pizza."

"Great idea," Sara says.

Peter punches his phone and comes up with a place that delivers, "One large pepperoni pizza on the way. You do eat pepperoni don't you? You're not a vegetarian anymore, are you?" I don't answer.

"Now, how about we talk, little sis," Peter sits on the sofa with me.

"What about?" I ask.

"You," he says.

"Me? And why I'm this way?" I say.

"Maybe."

"I'm this way because I was made from a bad egg." I have figured this out since I left the hospital. Maybe Dennis was made from a bad egg too.

"That's not the reason," Sara protests. "Nobody knows why this happens."

"I know," I say. "I was born this way. Old eggs. People used to die sooner. Fifty was old. Women dried up. Mother should never have had me so old. It's unnatural. Evil."

Peter runs his hand over his balding head maybe looking for the few remaining hairs. His mouth forms itself into a crooked smile. "Then you wouldn't be here at all," he says.

They need to understand what I'm saying. "That's why you and Sara didn't get this. You got younger eggs."

"No," Peter says. "We got lucky that's all."

"Mother had her old eggs removed," I explain. "They went inside her and scraped out all the eggs. They cooked them up in a dish for a while. Then they mixed them with sperm stuff from a bank. Then they stuck them back inside her. It was hidden in there, inside her eggs. Waiting for me. You escaped. I got caught. It's evil. They made me from old, sick stuff."

"I don't know what to say," Peter looks frustrated. He always thinks he knows what to say. "You're here. Got to make the most of it."

"Why didn't they make me the real way?" I say, moving the defrosting peas to my stomach.

"They couldn't," Peter stands up like he is about to give a lecture.

"Dad had lost all interest. But Mary Ellen still wanted a Florence. She worried all the time when she was pregnant...what a crazy thing she'd done. Having a child at fifty-four years old. I remember her saying, 'I'll be almost seventy when she's only fifteen...almost eighty when she's twenty-five.' But she wanted you."

"No one wants me now," I say it as coldly as I can. I don't want their pity. "No one wants *my* eggs." I push my stomach violently as if I could shove out what eggs might be there.

"I had a good brain." I throw the squishy bag of peas across the room. "I had lots of smart ideas. I can't put the ideas together any more."

MY BROTHER AND SISTER keep asking me if they are gone, the voices and the people in my head.

"Yes," I say. But then I tell them the truth. "Not always. Sometimes I still see them trying to talk to me. The drugs put my brain to sleep."

"Is your brain asleep now?" Peter asks.

"Some parts are awake. The thinking part is in pieces. The feeling part is like when your leg falls asleep."

"Yeah, I know that feeling," Peter says "It tingles, then wakes up slowly."

"I can't have children," I say. I think about Dennis, making babies with him.

"Nobody said that," Sara is quick to correct me. "I never heard any of the doctors say that. There is nothing wrong with you physically."

"I could give this to a child, and anyway, I couldn't take care of one. I can't take care of myself. You do everything, Sara."

"You say you don't feel, but I can tell you're sad," Peter says. "That's a feeling."

I consider this. It sounds logical. "Sad. I don't know. Does my face look sad?"

Peter admits that it doesn't. At best, it looks indifferent.

I GO UPSTAIRS FOR A REST. They say they'll tell me when the pizza arrives.

Once alone in my room I put my arms around my knees. First a low hum and then a song comes from me. "*Are you going away with no word of farewell, will there be not a trace left behind. Well, I could have loved you better, didn't mean to be unkind...*"

It sometimes works. I can make it happen. The moon is barely visible behind the clouds but I can still see her shining into me, giving me my voice back. As I sing she floats down from the grey sky into my room.

She listens to me sing.

"You have your mother's voice," she says.

"No," I whisper. "You aren't allowed to speak to me. They'll hear me talking to you. The pills make you silent. They told me the pills would make you silent. I can let you come down only if you are quiet."

"They also said the fear would be gone. But you're afraid of me," she laughs softly.

"I'm not. You have no body. You can't hurt me."

"I'm not here to hurt you," she says, but I can't trust her. I don't want her here anymore. I can make her come but I can't make her go away.

A quiet cry slips from my throat. I curl up on the floor with my arms protecting my head. "Please go away."

The woman in black takes her eyes off of me and looks around the room. "This is a nice house. So clean. Neat as a pin. Funny expression. Your mother used to say that. Thank you for bringing me here. I can't feel Mary Ellen here. But Sara is here. And Peter too."

"You won't hurt them?" I plead.

"No," she says. "I can't hurt them."

"Just me."

"Not you either," she says.

"But you tried to hurt me. I know. You pushed me off the bridge."

"You jumped," she laughs. "I never touched you."

"You told me to jump."

"That wasn't me." She walks around the room looking in the closet. "There were others there that night."

"Who are they?" I ask her. She knows more than all the doctors. The answers are right here.

"You tell me. You created us all separately. We don't know each other. You dress us alike, though. These black capes and hoods. Where did you get that?"

"I want to get rid of you!"

She sits on the bed next to me and takes hold of my arm to prevent me from running away. "Would you like to know who I am? You see, I'm harmless."

I'm afraid to say the words. "Are we the same person?"

"No, dear. Only to your mother. I died before you were born. I'm Florence too. Your aunt."

"You're dead. Long dead."

"You know me. We talk at night. I tell you how to make your

THE GOOD SIDE OF BAD

pictures. You're trying to find me in them. To see me. My face."

"You killed yourself."

"That's what they say," and again she laughs.

"You had this too, didn't you? You killed yourself just like I will one day. Just like Dennis did."

"You aren't going to kill yourself," she says with certainty.

I don't know if I feel relieved or sorry. "Can you see into the future? Do you really know that?"

"Well, to tell the truth, I don't. I could be wrong. If it helps any, I *didn't* kill myself. It may have looked that way, your mother certainly thought so, but no, it was an accident."

"I don't believe you."

"You don't believe me. You believe yourself. What you choose to believe."

"You died so young," I say.

"I was twenty-eight. But a pretty crazy twenty-eight. Back then, they didn't have these strong medicines you're taking now."

"But you're not twenty-eight now. You look at least seventy. Did you go on aging after you died?"

"Wouldn't that be something! Now that's a crazy idea if ever I heard one. No, you just choose to see me this way. I don't pick the way I look, you do."

"Why are you here now? "

"I wanted to say goodbye. Soon those pills of yours are going to kill me off for the second time. "

"You're going to leave me?" I say, feeling my hands go numb as I reach out for her. "I don't know who I'll be when you're gone."

"Don't worry about it too much. When you get older, you'll discover that nobody really knows who they are from day to day.

132

They just try and figure it out as they go along."

"But I need you. Now I know who you are. You're the one I look for in the face of the moon every night. Don't take away your face!"

Chapter 23

SARA

SUN SHINES ON THE pink rhododendrons I've planted outside the kitchen windows. April is always surprisingly beautiful. I've talked Peter into going to the arboretum with Florence and me to see the endless rows of azalea bushes in full bloom. For my money, the vibrant colors beat anything you can see in New England in the fall.

The smell of baking blueberry muffins fills the house. It's nine in the morning and I can hear Florence softly singing upstairs. She is awake and singing! Peter is in the living room reading the paper and I don't hear him swearing yet, so this has the potential of being a good day.

I bring Peter a cup of coffee just as Florence comes down the stairs. Her hair is pulled back tightly, giving her face a clean and innocent look. She is wearing a fresh pair of sweatpants and a green turtleneck sweater.

"I brought you something." Peter takes a camera out of his duffel bag and shows it to Florence. "This is the new Nikon D70. Top of the line. It has all sorts of things…digital matrix control…multiple exposure settings…"

Florence is staring right past him looking at a place in front of the bookcase as though she is waiting for an answer to a question.

"What are you looking at?" Peter tries to get her to focus on him.

"No," Florence says, turning to talk to the air in middle of the room. "Don't stay here. It's not safe. Go. Go away now."

Peter turns to me. "What do we do when this happens?"

"Wait. Talk to her gently," I say, assuring him this is a momentary thing. "It'll pass and Florence will be back with us." I'm used to these trance-like escapes. When she first came home, I wanted to call Dr. Richardson every time they happened. Ask him if I was giving her the medication correctly? Did she need more?

Florence sits on the floor and begins to sing. "*Summertime and the living is easy*." Softly at first then in a deep soulful voice.

"God, I forgot you could sing like that." Peter is astonished. "Lovely. You have a beautiful voice. Just like Mary Ellen's."

Suddenly Florence jumps up and runs from the room screaming. "You can't take away your face. Give me back my face."

Peter puts down the paper. "This is impossible. You can't live like this. She could hurt herself."

"I don't have a choice," I say. "It's not as bad as it seems. Can I get you a blueberry muffin?"

"Of course there's a choice," he addresses me like I'm a child. "There are places she can go. Places designed for people like her."

"Mentally ill people is what you mean."

"You're not facing it, Sara. That's what she is."

"She's so much more than that." I call upstairs to Florence. "Muffins coming out of the oven!" Then I turn to Peter. "You're not here. She can be warm and funny. "

"Yeah, in one minute and in the next she's running after invisible people. This may not be the healthiest place for her to live either. She needs qualified people who are trained to handle her."

"*Handle* her?" The expression makes me think of fruits being squeezed in the market. "She needs family to love her."

"There are several good places just north of the city," Peter says carefully.

"And how do you know that?" I challenge him. "You've already checked this out, haven't you?"

"I'm good at research," he says.

"An institution? You can't commit your sister to an institution."

"No, that's not what I'm talking about. These are supervised homes. Half-way houses. Just take at look at a few of these," he pulls out brochures from five or six places.

"No, I'm doing all right by myself," I tell him, pushing his brochures away. "You don't get to fly in here for a weekend and take charge. This is my decision. She stays with me."

"Fine. I'm just trying to help."

The phone rings.

"I'll get it," Peter says. "I left a message for Mother to call here when I arrived." He answers the phone.

"*Hello. Yes, this is her son. Yes, I'm in Seattle…Can you put her on the line…What?…When?…How bad?…Oh…This morning…No, thank you. Yes, I'll be back right away…Yes, please…You have my permission. Thank you. Goodbye.*" Peter doesn't move. The phone hangs in his right hand.

I'm afraid to speak. "What happened?"

His words come out in a monotone. "Mother had a heart attack early this morning. Her cleaning lady found her on the floor unconscious. They took her to the hospital."

"Oh my God. Oh. How is she? Is she going to be all right?"

Peter puts the phone down and goes back to the sofa. He stares at his hands as if he is looking for something that should be in them.

I wait.

"She died an hour ago. I just saw her last week. She was fine." I sit with him, taking his hands in mine. "I can't believe it," he says. "It's so sudden."

"I'm so sorry," I say, feeling guilty that at this moment I can't even bring a clear and recent picture of my mother to my mind. "I know you've been close to her in the last few years."

I look up and see that Florence is not in her room but sitting on the stairs listening to all this. She comes down to Peter. "Mother's dead?" she asks.

"Yes," Peter says, not looking at her.

"What do we feel?" Florence asks, and the absolute honesty of the question touches me.

"Numb, Florence," Peter says, looking up at her. "We feel numb."

Florence goes to the bookcase and finds a framed photo of Mary Ellen and Dad. She brings it to us. "I hadn't seen her in years," I say. "We've hardly spoken. But I've kept this. It's their wedding picture. She got married for the first time when she was thirty-five years old and she wore this strange dress. So filmy. She looks more like a ghost than a bride. See Florence, that was your mother nineteen years before you were born."

"She sang to the children," Florence says.

"What children?" Peter asks.

"The ones she forgot. Us." Florence runs a finger across Mother's face in the photo. We three sit in silence, and then Florence sings, halting at first, then beautifully.

"I am the mountain, I am the sky. I am the river. I fly and fly. I am a part of everything I see. I am of nature. It is of me."

"We're orphans now," Florence says after a moment.

"Only children can be orphans. Not adults," Peter says.

"Now we all go back together," Florence says, taking charge.

"You're not well enough to go to a funeral," Peter smiles at her.

"All three of us have to go," Florence insists. "We have to say goodbye."

Chapter 24

PETER

THE ONLY GOOD SIDE of this bad situation is that I don't have to fly alone. I'm grateful to have Sara in the seat next to me, and even Florence on the aisle seat gives me some comfort. At least this time if the plane goes down on my return to New York I'm not going out alone. I have family and we're all going together. If only Florence doesn't freak out somewhere over the middle of the country and see angels flying past the windows.

Who would come to the funeral? I wonder. Did Mary Ellen have friends in Connecticut? Are there family members I don't know about, or past friends to notify? Did she want to be buried or cremated? Was there a trust or a will? So many questions and I don't have the answers. And there is no one to ask.

Sara is surprised that I know so little about our mother's life since she had returned to live in Connecticut. I hadn't ever taken her to a doctor, visited her when she had friends over, or had met her neighbors. Nothing. It turns out I know pretty much nothing.

"We'll find an address book," Sara suggests. "We'll call all the names in it find out who they are and how they know Mother."

This strikes me as an arduous task. I have no desire to make cold calls to a bunch of strangers tell them Mary Ellen has died and then casually ask them, oh, by the way, how did you know my mother? My approach was much simpler.

"Why don't we just put a notice in the obituaries section in the local paper? All those old people probably read the obits every day to make sure that anybody who's died was older and sicker than they were."

Florence is quiet most of the flight, lost in her own world. Then she surprises me, saying, "I don't think we should burn her." I know what she means but the choice of words is unfortunate.

Ironically my own will requests that I be cremated. The ashes are not my concern. Whoever survives me can do whatever they want with them. Why had I never asked Mary Ellen about what she wanted? Maybe the thought of Mary Ellen as mortal seemed impossible. She ran her own life and allowed no one to know where the money or jewels were hidden, not even if there were any of these things. Her finances were pretty much a mystery to me. Did she even own the house she lived in? Where did her income come from? Was it sad or good that I know so little about my mother's life? Sad that I cared too little to ask for the details, or good that right up to the end Mary Ellen was pretty much in charge of her own life?

Once we arrive in Connecticut decisions get made quickly. People are called, notices are posted, a funeral is scheduled. We check out the cemetery.

"I'd forgotten how beautiful it is in spring," Sara says. We drive pass rows of gravestones, but Sara is looking only at the flowers. "Can you believe this!" We're surrounded by woods filled with poppies and yellow lilies. "Look, there's blue lupine. They must have just bloomed all over Southern New England." The sun bouncing off fields of color gives her a flicker of hope. "Maybe things will start getting better."

I stop the car just before turning up the lane to the gravesite. Sara and Florence get out, walk up the hillside and pick wildflowers. I remember how Mary Ellen had pushed away my store-bought flowers. They had to come from the ground on her hillside. These are the only flowers she would want us to bury with her.

Sara is pointing out the different flowers to Florence She knows the names of all of them. They're all just colors to me, except maybe the basics like daisies or roses.

"Look, these are trout lilies and this is bloodroot." Sara the teacher can be found in any situation.

When we were kids, maybe seven and nine, Sara would sneak into my bedroom at night and we'd try and stay awake as long as we could, holding on to the last moments of the day. Her favorite way to keep sleep at bay was the flower game. We took turns naming flowers that grew in the neighbor's garden. Funny how that memory comes back to me now. The trick was to learn them in alphabetical order. She made up a song so that I would remember the flower's names. "A for asters, B for begonias, C for Calla lilies, D for daisies" The rest is lost. It's the only girly thing I remember doing with Sara in our youth. Most of the time I forced her to play war with my metal soldiers.

As I watch my two sisters climb the hill, I remember Mary Ellen riding up here with me, then taking her horse into a gallop when we reached the valley on the other side. What a powerful woman she was.

"They're all gone," I tell Sara.

"What's all gone?" she asks.

"The unanswered questions that haunted me all my life. Did

she care at all about us? Was she proud of me? And the real biggie: did she love me?

"I'm sure the answer to all those is yes…she did on some level," Sara says, admiring a yellow flower that she tells me is a columbine. She picks one in red and shows it to Florence. They move away from me up the hill where the spring flowers are even more abundant. And I realize that Sara let these questions go a long time ago. As a child she had cried for losing Mother every time Mary Ellen went on the road. She had lost her so often that maybe this final loss has no power over her. We had no idea who would arrive that morning at the small chapel at the cemetery. Would there be enough seats? Would anyone come?

A handful of people arrive. A few neighbors, Henry, who took care of her horse, and her dentist. The service is simple, I say a few words then Florence sings "Amazing Grace." Her voice could fill a cathedral, much less this tiny chapel. Sara and I sit in the front pew clasping hands. Unexpected tears wet my face. Am I crying for Mary Ellen or for Florence? Or maybe it's just the song, the music, the soaring emotion it invokes?

"You did her proud," I say to Florence, and surprisingly, she allows me to take her in my arms.

We bury Mary Ellen in the village cemetery not a mile from the place she had called home for the last fifteen years. Florence places the flowers she and Sara had gathered on the hillside.

THE THREE OF US SPEND two days together going through papers and looking at old pictures of ourselves as children. We find shoeboxes full of photos, most of them probably taken by our father, but at least Mary Ellen hadn't thrown them out. They never made it into frames or picture albums. Our young faces grew up in shoeboxes. One day, I think, I'll be in one of these shoeboxes, my whole being reduced to ashes that will fit inside this box. Then I will disappear into the wind somewhere, my speck of time gone.

"What do we do with all this?" Sara is overwhelmed. "How do we decide what to keep and what to throw out?"

"Easy." Maybe the only thing I have in common with Mary Ellen is the ability to make a quick decision. "We all just take what we want and the rest gets tossed."

We hadn't expected any inheritance but we also hadn't expected all the outstanding bills. It turned out Mary Ellen wasn't as in control of her life as it appeared. A good piece of it could be found in the debt she charged to her credit cards.

"What are we going to do about all these bills," Sara asks?

"You forget, dear sister," I say. "I'm rich. At least I was the last time I looked."

Before we leave for the airport, we go back to Mary Ellen's grave site one more time. I feel like I'm walking in a dream as we thread our way past grave markers to find our mother. "There she is," Florence calls out as if she is on a treasure hunt and has just found the prize. She walks on ahead of Sara and me.

When we reach the site, we see Florence sitting next to the grave and crying. Sara and I look at each other, not knowing what to do. The medications have pretty much dulled Florence's emotions. She hasn't reacted at all to Mother's death until now. Sara turns me away so that Florence can be alone.

"She lived here with Mother for two years after college, so maybe there was a bond we didn't know about," Sara whispers.

"Mother made Florence live in the barn, not in the main house.

They hardly spoke to each other," I remind her.

"How do you know? You weren't there." Sara is right. I only have Florence's words to go on and I know now how unreliable they are. Maybe there was a connection between them, but Mother never seemed to care that Florence moved out. She never even asked about her.

When I turn back, I see Florence lying on the ground next to the grave site. She is softly humming one of Mary Ellen's favorite songs, "Blue Bayou."

"We have to go," I say.

"Not yet," Florence says softly. "We are singing together."

SUMMER

2008

Chapter 25

PETER

ROKERS AND TRADERS WHO are usually glued to their screens watching the market are now simultaneously watching CNN and MSNBC. The financial world is an unpredictable Category Five storm looking like it's moving in on us at top speed. Every day another bombshell hits the news. Scandals are everywhere. The country's largest banks are scrambling to stay alive. The sub-prime house of cards is starting to fall apart.

I decide to shed some weight. I drop positions on half of my holdings not caring about the big losses I'm incurring. My Porsche was in a garage two blocks from my apartment where I was paying $250 a month for the privilege of letting it sit unused. I had bought it to take women on weekends upstate. I'd planned on an hour's visit with Mother and then a few days at a B&B getting laid. Now Mother is gone, and so it seems is my sex life. There isn't time for anything now. We all come into the office every day to see if we still have jobs.

The poker games are over. We just get together to drink. It's strange that I have spent so many hours, mostly with Patrick and Don, discussing our investments, our business conquests, and I really don't know anything about them personally. Oh, I know they are both married and even that there are some children in the picture, but wives and kids were never the topics of our conversations. They were all about the game, the next deal. And now the next deal is getting deadly serious.

On June 19th, we're at Cipriani's drinking and considering our options when Patrick breaks the bad news, "I just heard that two of Bear Stearns ex-fund managers have been arrested by the FBI. *Arrested*, for God's sake."

"What are the charges?" Don asks, unable to keep the fear out of his voice.

"Fraud," Patrick says, with the same intensity as if he had said murder.

"Okay," I say. "So what has this got to do with us? We're clean. We're clear."

"You don't get it, Peter," Patrick says, downing another whiskey. "They were arrested for their fraudulent role in the sub-prime mortgage collapse. They misrepresented the fiscal health of their funds to investors publicly while privately withdrawing their own money."

"So they're assholes and also stupid," I say.

"What I'm asking here," says Patrick, "is how is this any different than what we are doing? Is the FBI sitting outside our door?"

"We haven't misrepresented the value of our funds to investors," I say, knowing I'm on very thin ice here. "How could we when *we* don't even know the value of our funds? For Christ's sake, Patrick, lay it on the line here: do you even know what the hell you been selling for the past five years?"

"I haven't a clue," Don chimes in. "The value of these funds is so volatile. It's all a moving target. There's no single day when you can put an absolute value on any of them. But fraud! The three of us? We didn't intentionally misrepresent any of it, did we?" he looks at Patrick and me for redemption. We don't offer any.

"Of course we did," Patrick says. "We can't suddenly declare amnesia here. The three of us have been sitting around a poker table trying to best each other with the volume and sheer audacity of our sales. Here, with my fourth whiskey, I declare only to the two of you, that I have talked my way through sales that would never have happened if I'd been completely open about what I knew."

"So are we going to jail?" Don asks a little too cavalierly.

"Maybe, maybe not," Patrick says. "It depends on how deep this thing goes, how many investigators the Feds have, and whether they go all the way down the food chain to Lambert & Hall."

"We may not be going to jail," I interject. "But we're probably going to hell. I'm still selling funds to investors while privately withdrawing my own money from everything that even smells of risk."

"So that's it," Don says. "We're the guys that Tom Wolfe wrote about. You know, the *Bonfire of the Vanities*. Well, we're the new vanities and this market collapse is our bonfire."

"What's the game plan?" Patrick asks. "Do we sell everything and get out of town? Or do we hold tight and hope all of this blows over? They hang a few of the big fish, ignore us and after a little while, we're all back in business again."

"Or maybe it's not as bad here as at Bear Stearns," Don offers. "Sure, there's going to be a lot of blood in the streets but maybe we're solid."

"I hate to bust your bubble," I say. "But the only hedge fund managers who are going to survive this are the ones who saw it coming. The ones that knew Moody's credit ratings were full of shit and bet against the sub-prime mortgages, running to gold. That's not L & H."

"So it's over," Don says.

"Not until the fat lady sings," Patrick laughs, lifting his glass for a toast. "So far we are still fat and we are not singing."

Chapter 26

SARA

T'S A FEW MONTHS AFTER Mother's funeral and life has calmed down somewhat. Florence is staying on her medications, accepting her life in my home. She doesn't do yoga anymore. She doesn't do much of anything. She sleeps a good part of the day. I never hear her talking to the air.

Since my summer school classes are cancelled, I am out of work with nothing to do but watch over Florence. This might be all right for the summer; I have money saved up, but what if I don't get hired back in the fall? I will have to find a job. Doing what? The only thing I want to do is teach. What other skills do I have? What can I put on a resume that would impress anyone?

Now as I push my cart down a narrow aisle in Wal-Mart past an endless selection of sugar-laden cereals I feel the depression that comes with moving down a few rungs on the social ladder. I pass the turkey dinners with brown gravy at nine million calories a pop. Shopping is no longer an adventure with exotic cheeses and chili-flavored chocolates offered for tasting. Whole Foods is in the past. Shopping is now a necessary task full of tiny disappointments and sad decisions.

Have I really become so poor that I have to consider whether double-ply toilet paper is worth the extra dollar or if I could get by on single ply? With scalding guilt, I toss two bags of Oreo cookies into my basket. I would never feel this bad had they been fresh from the in-store bakery. I have to get back to Whole Foods.

I entertain the idea that my economic challenges are all in my mind. I could still substitute teach. I'm not broke, so why do I feel the need to watch every penny?

AT LEAST I CAN GET MYSELF together. That seems like a good place to start. I haven't paid attention to my appearance in so many years that I have no idea where to begin. Eight-year-old children don't care what you look like as long as you're nice, take them on great field trips and make their learning interesting. And the other teachers look just like me, a little bit frumpy, a little overweight and completely uninterested in their own appearance.

The idea of going to yoga with Florence had crossed my mind when she first moved into my house. But she was too shaken by the death of that poor boy in the hospital. She never wanted to talk about what happened, so I didn't ask. It must have been a terrible thing to see. I wonder if she is afraid she might do the same thing to herself.

Since Florence has no interest, I decide to go to yoga by myself. There is a little studio called New Life Yoga just a mile from the house. The instructor is an incredibly handsome and well put-together guy in his mid-twenties. My years of celibacy haunt me as I watch him demonstrate the poses. His body moves so effortlessly from one pose to another that I find myself having sexual fantasies about him all during the class. It is fun having this fantasy life, and the yoga feels good too. I am the oldest one in the room. I imagine that all the other students, mostly fit young female bodies, are having lovely sexual fantasies about our lithe instructor too. At first I am stiff and it is difficult for me to do most of the class. I keep going and after a few weeks I feel stronger and more flexible. It is a joy to use my body again after I had allowed it to sit unused for so many years.

Today the young instructor, Sean, comes over to me and touches me low on my spine, adjusting my position. His hand gently presses my hot skin. He then moves on to the next student. I freeze, afraid that if I move I will jump up and grab him.

As he walks away from me, my eye catches the mirrors that line the side of the room and I'm greeted with an unwelcome reflection of myself. Forget worrying about when I had become poor. The more important question was when had I become so dumpy? My navy blue sweatshirt doesn't fall over curves but rather over bunches. My face, which I had always thought of as mildly cute, is cracking into pieces right before my eyes. Lines run in all directions: out on my brow, down from my nose. And my hair. What color is it anyway? What was between blonde and grey? This wasn't supposed to happen for another ten years. I'm only forty. Did divorce speed up the aging process? Does living alone, without anyone to comment on your appearance, push you off the cliff into middle age? Was this person in the glass actually me?

After class, I go directly to a beauty salon and have them get rid of my non-descript hair color.

I walk out of there a brilliant blonde without a trace of gray.

Chapter 27

FLORENCE

HEAT RISES. IT COMES UP from the kitchen and living room up the stairs past the den, past Sara's room, what used to be the master bedroom, the guest bedroom, and then it seeps into my room. At each step of the way, it goes up a degree.

I lie on the bed naked with a cold washcloth across my forehead. I hear Sara talking to people on the phone about this heat wave. Breaking all records. Ninety-eight degrees in Seattle, unbelievable. No air conditioning in these old houses. This is an old city in what is supposed to be a cool climate. Weather. Weather. It is always too hot or too cold. Doesn't anyone have a memory? It's July, it's hot. So simple. Nine months of the year it is cold and rainy, a few weeks in the summer it is too hot. It's this way every year; it never changes and yet they talk about it every year as if it's all a big surprise.

If I don't get out of bed and get dressed soon, Sara will be up here nagging at me, pushing me to get moving. It doesn't matter to me if I stay in bed all day but she can't stand to see it. She says I'm wasting my life, that I'll never get better if I don't get out into the world and *do* something.

Do something. Is that what would make my life better? Doing. There's nothing I want to do. I think about Dennis. I think about him all the time. Why did he do it that morning? Maybe he just felt he had nothing left to do. But doing something, anything was too random, nonspecific and unlikely. You've got to have something to stick around for. And I had thought that something was me. The something he could do, that we could do, was be together in a world we both understood. I guess I wasn't enough reason for him. And if he could do it, why wouldn't I?

"Florence," Sara yells up the stairs. "You've got to get out of bed. It's almost eleven o'clock. I've got eggs on. You know the doctor told you that you have to eat protein in the morning. Please come downstairs now. I've got to leave in a few minutes."

Sara keeps a list of everything the doctor says I should do. I see him once a week, so Sara has an endless supply of things to add to her list. It includes what I should eat, what I should wear, who I should see, how much I should sleep, what I should read. For the last few weeks the doctor and Sara have teamed up to bring structure to my life. Not only am I supposed to do all the things on their list, but I have to do them at specific times of day and for specific amounts of time. Structure. Continuity. Routine. I hated all those things before. They were never a part of my life. Why would making them the key to my health make any sense now?

I don't have the energy to fight them. I get out of bed and dress in what has become my uniform, black sweatpants and a sleeveless T-shirt. Downstairs Sara is laying out a plate that would put a first-class restaurant's breakfast to shame. Something she calls coddled eggs, English muffins with homemade blueberry jam, Canadian bacon, cinnamon buns, fresh squeezed orange juice. Just looking at it makes me want to vomit.

"I'm going to Starbucks," I say, leaving the breakfast sitting untouched at the table. I can see Sara is disappointed that I can't appreciate all the work she has done, that I won't sit with her, telling her how delicious it all is.

"Okay," she says, at least relieved that I have a destination outside the house.

For the last two weeks I have walked three blocks down the hill to Starbucks, ordered a simple coffee, black, and sat at a corner table for an hour sipping it until it is cold. This is structure. I do the same thing each day and it seems to give Sara some hope.

I don't read a newspaper or a book. I watch people come and go, talk with one another, laugh, reach across the table to touch each other's hands. Today there are men in suits and women in business clothes talking excitedly about things financial. I overhear fragments of their conversations and imagine what it is like to care about the things that they're talking about.

Two suits and a blue dress sit down at the table across from me. Their conversation is so animated, their eyes so full of expression, their arms waving in the air as they speak. They must be talking about something fun, perhaps an adventure they shared together, their weekends away from the office. But instead all this excitement seems to be about bad things.

"My broker is an idiot," one of the suits says. "He couldn't predict what was happening if he could channel Nostradamus. My plan is to do the opposite of everything he tells me to do. If he says sell a fund, I buy more of it. If he tells me about a great stock, I quickly send out an e-mail to everybody I care about and tell them to stay as far away from it as possible. I tell you, this new strategy is working out pretty well."

The other suit and the blue dress laugh loudly and quickly

jump in to add their own stories of disgust and disappointment with their brokers.

"I tell you," the blue dress says, "we haven't begun to see the bottom of this. My daughter and her husband bought a house with an interest-only loan." The three of them laugh again as if this is the craziest thing they have ever heard. "I mean, really," she says, "they have absolutely no credit. No bank should have given them a loan. Take it from me, we're headed into a big-time depression."

I try to make sense of their conversation. If the economy is falling apart and we're going to have a big depression, why is it all so funny? Is this just some hysterical energy they're blowing off with each other? Or maybe they're just trying to show off how smart, witty and in the know they are.

I'm glad when they finish their coffee and leave. A young couple replaces them, talking in whispers that I can't overhear. They seem so focused on each other that I find myself preferring the depression people.

My structured hour has passed and I can walk the three blocks back home.

"DID YOU HAVE A NICE CUP of coffee?" Sara greets me when I get back. School got out a week ago, so Sara is off work. She's home every day. It was so much easier when I had the house to myself. I could go back to sleep whenever I wanted. Now that she is off for the summer, she wants to plan little outings for us. Those are also on the doctor's list of things I should be doing. I'm not prepared for the big plan she hits me with today.

"It's going to be in the high nineties again tomorrow. Much too hot to stay in the house," she says, working up to telling me her big plan.

"It's too hot to go outside," I say.

"Not if we're on the water. I booked a special adventure for us tomorrow."

"God, you sound like you're talking to one of your eight-year-olds. *A special adventure.*" I mock her.

"That's okay, let's be nine together tomorrow. Look," she puts the newspaper in front of me and points out the article she wants me to read. "One of the Puget Sound resident orca whale pods has been spotted in the Straits of Juan de Fuca." I can see where this is leading.

"Tomorrow morning we're catching a whale watching boat off Pier 39. It's a day trip but we'll make it all the way up into the Straits and if we're lucky well see killer whales. "

"Do I have veto power?" I ask.

"Come on, Florence, it will be fun, I promise you. It's going to be a gorgeous sunny day. Even if we don't see whales, we'll stay cool and have a good time. I've lived in Seattle all these years and I've never taken a boat into the Straits."

"I get it. This is something you've always wanted to do. Does it matter if it's not something I want to do?"

"But that's just the problem, you don't do anything. You don't know what you want to do. So this summer we are just going to do things until you find out what you like."

"I like sleeping," I say without a trace of sarcasm in my voice. My sleep used to be full of dreams. The antipsychotic drugs have put an end to that. I was afraid that I would dream about Dennis. The bad part, seeing him on the floor of the hospital. All that blood. I've wanted to see him in my dreams, to remember him holding me in the hospital. But I had to be sure that if he entered my dreams he would be whole, talking with me, touching my hair. He never came inside my head when I was asleep. Nothing did. Oblivion. Darkness. Quiet. That's what sleep offers me. That is the something I've wanted to do, sleep.

I feel sorry for Sara; her days look as empty as mine. She doesn't know what to do with herself since they canceled summer school. And now there is even a question as to whether she will have a job in the fall. This great depression I heard them talking about in the coffee shop is sneaking into our house. Teachers are losing their jobs and Sara is losing her identity. She has done so much for me, taking me in, keeping me alive and away from the hospital, that I feel I owe her some obedience. If she wants to go look at a bunch of orca whales, I can go with her. I don't have to do anything, just sit on a boat and look out at the water.

EVERYTHING IS MORE complicated than we think it will be. First, we cannot find a place to park. Downtown Seattle is packed with tourists. They crowd Pike Place Market and the whole wharf. I suggest we give up the whole idea but Sara is insistent. We drive around the crowded blocks and look for anywhere to put the car.

"We should have taken the water taxi over," Sara says. "It goes right from West Seattle to the wharf."

"That would have been a good idea if you'd had it an hour ago. Maybe we forget this plan for today go home and take the water taxi next week?"

"You're not getting out of this," Sara says. 'This will be good for you," She finally pulls into a spot that barely accommodates even her Mini Cooper.

Once on the boat, I have to admit things do pick up. I sit in the bow and feel the wind blow across my face and I can smell the sea. If Sara would stop talking I think I could quietly fall asleep and then my pleasure would be complete. I would be doing something.

It takes us about two hours to motor out to the Straits of Juan de Fuca. There are snacks and more importantly a bar on board and it seems that most of these day cruisers have a drink in their hand, a beer, a glass of wine, a margarita. If Sara wasn't here I'd have a couple of beers myself. Unfortunately that's on her list of what I can't do; no alcohol. It doesn't mix with the drugs.

There are suddenly screams of delight. A tiny woman in a yellow dress shouts, "Look, a dolphin off the starboard bow." Ten minutes later two more dolphins arrive and ride our wake. You would think that all aboard had just been given a million-dollar prize, their excitement is so intense.

Sara is hanging over the rail like the rest of the passengers watching the dolphins play. Next to her is a tall good-looking man in his mid-forties, wearing a blue Mariners sweatshirt. He is talking to Sara, pointing at the dolphins, smiling and laughing. Sara is smiling back. There is something different about her. She looks thinner and fitter. Her face seems wide open, more alive then I have ever seen her. When did this change happen? Have I forgotten how to notice when people change? I stare at her as she talks to the blue sweatshirt and I'm surprised to discover that in this little moment, my sister is pretty.

I wonder if Dennis was ever in a boat in the middle of the Sound looking over the side at the churning water and smiling. If I get too close to the rail, I think I'll be tempted to slip my legs over it and slide into the water myself. It looks so cold and inviting.

Now everyone is pointing far in the distance at a spout of water. "There they are," a boy shouts. "The whales!"

The captain of the boat slows our engines. His voice comes on over a loudspeaker, "Listen up everyone, once we spot whales, we have to stop where we are to see where they're going. It's illegal to bring a boat closer than one hundred yards from the whales."

We are dead in the water for at least a half hour before the whales start moving in our direction. I begin to see them breaking the surface of the water with their perfect black and white bodies. The captain is back on the loudspeaker destroying the magic of the moment with his scripted information. "Orcas, or killer whales as they are commonly known, are not vegetarians like gray or blue whales. They are the predators of the sea."

Everyone gets quiet as the whales approach the boat. I count at least twelve of them swimming along our starboard side. I am shocked at how beautiful they are. Then I see one leap out of the water, its whole body flying in the air before me. How is it possible with all of that enormous weight that it can soar above the surface? Cameras are going off all around me. Why, I think, why would you want to miss this moment by putting a lens between yourself and these magnificent animals?

The largest of the whales moves in closest to the boat. He can't be more than twenty feet away. A thunderous noise rocks me as a fountain of water comes out of his blowhole. His head turns and for just an instant I see one of his eyes looking straight into mine. I want to jump into the water and fly with him. I want to cry and be free of my crazy body, my sick mind. No tears come. There is still a wall of drugs between me and feeling. And in that minute I know I have no choice. I can't live in a fog any longer. I reach into my pocket and find the little vial of pills I'm supposed to take. I uncap the bottle, put my hand over the rail, and watch as the little white pills fall into the sea.

No more little white pills. I'm going to swim free again, no matter how dangerous the waters.

Chapter 28

SARA

I N LATE JULY EVERYTHING changes. Shortly after I took Florence to see the whales, the switch that had been turned off by the antipsychotic drugs clicked back on again. My sister's behavior reverts back to the way it was before she first went into the hospital.

Florence is frantically taking photographs throughout my house. She spends hours arranging random objects into compositions before they are ready for her camera. She pins up her pictures of fruit and vegetables over the living room walls. There are a few portraits she must have taken at the coffee shop, but the people are faceless. Their heads are turned away from the camera, bent or in shadow.

"Did you bring me oranges?" she asks, ready to accuse me of negligence if I have forgotten one of her requests.

"Yes, there in that bag." At least oranges are ordinary and easy to obtain. I've tried to bring her all the things she's wanted for her photographs. But sometimes it's not easy. Last week she wanted a perfect orange starfish and an old weathered birdhouse.

I hand her four oranges.

"Oh, perfect. These are so bright."

"What does it matter if they're bright or even if they're orange?" I ask. "You only shoot your pictures in black and white."

"Black and white shows the intensity of color without the pain," she says, not answering my question.

She has spread her stuff all over the coffee table, the sofa and the living room floor. I have given up trying to keep my home neat. I'm afraid to move anything in case I upset her.

"Are these new?" I ask her, looking closely at the still-life photos. She ignores me. "These are good. Maybe you could think about showing them to someone."

"They're only for me," she snaps.

"The compositions are interesting. How did you get this egg to stand up on end like that?" I pick up one of the eggs she has lying on the table and try to make it stand on end. I fail. "Show me how you did that."

Florence takes the egg from my hand, breathes on the wider end and carefully places it standing up. I try the same trick but can't make the egg stand again.

"You have magic powers," I tease her.

She is suddenly wild. "It's not magic. Anybody can do it. I don't have any powers. I hate it when you say that. Leave me alone."

"Calm down. This is what the doctor told you would happen if you stopped taking your pills."

She is defiant. "I take them. I take them. I take them."

"It doesn't help to lie," I say in a low voice.

"I don't lie."

Before she can stop me, I run up the stairs to her room and look on the night stand for her meds. They're not there.

"Where are you going," she screams. "Stay out of my room."

I return empty-handed. "I can't find your pills. What did you do with them? You have to take them."

"No. They make it all go away. All the color goes away."

"Please, just tell me where they are," I plead.

She throws the glass of water she's holding in my face. "No. I hate you. Leave me alone."

"I will. You know you can always move to that group house we visited. Then you won't have to put up with me any more," I tell her.

"I hate that place. Everyone there is crazy."

"Maybe they can take better care of you than I can. "

"I don't want to go there!" She turns contrite. "I'm sorry about the egg. I'll show you how to do it. Don't take me to a crazy house. Sara, I'm sorry, please."

"It's not a crazy house," I'm determined to be strong. "It's a beautiful place where everyone is learning how to take care of themselves. You liked it when we visited last month. The magnolias were in bloom. Remember you loved those flowers."

"I liked the flowers, not the people."

"The people were very nice to you."

"It's an institution where people go in and never come out," she says demoralized.

"It's a half-way house."

"Half-way to where? "

"I've tried my best, Florence. But it's your choice. If you move I'll come and see you all the time. So will Peter."

"I make Peter depressed. He doesn't know what to do with me. You want to get rid of me so you can go out."

"I want you to get well."

"I can't get well."

"Then I want you to get better," I say hopefully.

"I'm staying here."

"Okay."

"You're going out tonight?"

"Yes."

"Where are you going? You never used to go anywhere."

"Well, I am now," I say. "And I have you to thank for it. I'm going to a movie with Sean, your yoga teacher. I've been going to his class for a couple of months. We go out, mostly for coffee. It's not like we're dating or anything. We're just friends. I think."

"Friends, my ass," she spits the words at me. "You're sleeping with him, aren't you?"

"There's more film in the bag on the table," I say. It's my chance to ignore one of *her* questions. "It's a beautiful day. We don't get that many perfect days. Why don't you go outside and take pictures?"

"Why don't you stop telling me what to do?"

I'm done. "Great idea. Stay inside. Do whatever you want. It's your life."

"It's *not* my life. Not the one I was supposed to have. It doesn't belong to me. It just happens. The days happen."

"Stop feeling so sorry for yourself," I snap back at her. "Days happen to all of us."

"You get to think about them in advance. Make them happen the way you want."

"Sometimes," I say. "Not often in the last nine months."

"Because I'm here," she says quietly, sitting on the floor. "I'm in your way. It's the same as when I lived with Peter. You'll end up hating me too."

"I need to get dressed," I tell her. "I haven't got time for this right now." She throws an egg across the room. The small driftwood boat that Peter made me as a child falls to the floor.

"Stop it. Go away!" Florence screams at the air. "I want to go away. Be free of me too. How can I go away from *me*? No, leave me alone. Go away. I don't care. I want my life back. I don't want to live in a home for sick people.

"What's the point of this? Why am I doing it?" Florence starts tearing up her photos. "There's nothing here. No life here. Just stillness with those damn pills. Nothing moves. I can't make things move. I need *them* to move me and the pills made *them* go away. I won't take pills. I want to be happy. See, I'm happy now.

"The people I see, they aren't all hurting me. Stay and listen to me, Sara. Some of them were nice. Aunt Florence is here. Sometimes she's kind to me."

This stops me. "You see your Aunt Florence? She died long before you were even born."

"She had this too, didn't she?"

"How can you know that?" I'm frightened now.

"Just tell me!" She looks at me with desperation in her eyes. "Please tell me, I need to know."

"Yes. I guess so." I sit on the floor with her. "Doctors knew so little about it back then."

"You think she killed herself, but she didn't," Florence whispers to me.

"You never knew her."

"I know her *now*," Florence says, jumping up and twirling around. She looks at empty space in the middle of the room. "You drove your car into a tree just like I did," she says to the room.

She turns back to me to explain. "But no one told her to do it. It was an accident. A real accident."

Her wild dance turns her back to the empty space. "You dropped a cigarette on your lap and lost control of the car."

"You're making that up," I say. I feel like I'm in the middle of someone else's unsteady dream. "Nobody knew how she died. She was alone."

"She told me that I'm not going to kill myself either. So you don't have to send me away. Here," she gives the camera to me. "Take a picture of me. See if I'm alone. Come on. Look at me Sara. I'm right here. Take a picture."

I don't know what else to do, so I comply, but just as I'm about to take the picture, Florence grabs the camera back. "No, I'll be black and white. You'll make me gray forever."

She begins tearing her pictures from the wall. I try to stop her, to calm her down. She slaps me across the face. "Don't stop me. You can't stop me." I grab her arms to stop the attack. We both stumble, falling to the floor.

"I'm not going to hurt you," I say.

"I want my life back," Florence yells. "I want my life back. The one I was supposed to have."

"Me too," I say, holding Florence down. "I want my marriage back. That was the life I was supposed to have. A husband and children. It's not going to happen. Peter wants his life back. The life he was supposed to have with Lydia. So maybe those aren't the lives we were supposed to have. There is no 'supposed to.' What makes us so special that we get to say what life owes us? We've got to stop wishing for the life we wanted and start living the life we've got. This is it. Right now, you and me in this house. Fighting each other.

"I'm tired of it," I say, breaking away from Florence. "I'm tired of feeling sorry for you. I'm tired of feeling sorry for me. I'm going to get dressed."

I leave Florence in the living room and go upstairs, feeling sick that I'm not up to the task of dealing with her. The phone rings and I hurry into the bedroom to pick it up. Doctors, psychiatrists, pharmacists are usually at the other end of the line giving me test results, blood results and instructions on Florence's medications. I'm taken off guard when a male voice at the other end of the phone has an entirely different agenda in mind.

"Hey," his cheery voice says. "How are you doing?"

"Okay," I say, finding the voice familiar.

"This is Charlie. Remember me? We met on that whale watching cruise a few weeks ago."

Remember him! I dreamed about him for the whole next week. My erotic fantasies of Sean the yoga guy had effortlessly transferred over to Charlie the whaleboat guy.

Talking to strange men has never been my forte, not that many opportunities have been offered to me over the years. But even if someone had tried to start a conversation with me I'm sure I would have brushed him off and never realized there was any potential in the moment. So why had it been different on the boat?

It had been such a perfect day. Florence was quiet but she had seemed almost happy out on the Straits of Juan de Fuca. And then there had been the whales, oh my God, the whales. Everyone just lit up inside when they swam around us and leapt into the air. So when this tall lovely man standing next to me shared my excitement I forgot all my reserve and handed him my phone number. I don't think I've given a strange man my phone number since I was in college. I never expected him to call. And now here he is, at the other end of the line, asking me if I would like to have dinner.

I don't hesitate a moment.

"Yes," I say. "Yes, that would be wonderful."

Chapter 29

PETER

T HE LIVES OF MY SISTERS fall into the background at the
beginning of September. When Fannie Mae and Freddie Mac
are taken under the government's wing, I know it's all over.
Almost every home mortgage lender and Wall Street bank relied on
them. Investors worldwide owned over five trillion dollars of debt
securities backed by them. It will only be a matter of days before
Lehman falls and then the whole banking system.

The panic at Lambert & Hall escalates by the hour. In a matter
of days I know that I'll be obsolete. Company funds are on the
block for a fraction of their previous value. What a laugh, I think;
they never really had a "previous worth." It was all a house of cards.
Everything the talking heads on CNBC are saying is true and it's
only the beginning.

Patrick and I are dealing with all this by meeting at the crack of
dawn every day in Central Park and running. We used to be running buddies ten years ago when we first met at L & H but Patrick
quit, saying it was too hard. Besides he didn't plan on needing his
body in great shape to attract women once he had money. The body
or the money, he'd said, but he didn't need both. He put on twenty
pounds and about seven inches in his waist and prided himself on

now looking like a real Wall Street banker.

Running was never about staying fit or thin for me. It was the challenge that turned me on, achieving something. I wanted to go farther and faster each day, and if I was going to run with Patrick, that meant running slower and shorter distances. We never ran so fast that we couldn't keep up a conversation. We both needed that early morning debrief of the financial meltdown. I figured I could run again in the evening on my own as fast as I wanted.

We meet at the north end of the reservoir at six o'clock and stretch our legs before starting. "Boy, Merrill Lynch really dodged a bullet," Patrick says as we hit our stride. "They got under Bank of America's umbrella just in time."

"Too bad Lehman Brothers couldn't find a buyer. The wires say they filed for bankruptcy protection this morning," I say, beginning to feel that sense of release that running always gives me.

"I don't think we can even comprehend how deep this can go. I'll bet it ends up burning every broker on Wall Street."

"Forget the brokers," I say, consciously shortening my stride so that I won't leave Patrick in my dust. "For that matter forget Wall Street. This is going to burn everybody with a shaky mortgage in America. This is going to be a middle-class crash."

"Do you know any?" Patrick says, already starting to get out of breath.

"Any what?" I ask.

"Middle-class people?"

"Aren't we middle-class?" I ask.

"Are you kidding? Middle-class people don't make the kind of money we do."

"So you're saying we're upper-class?"

"Sure," he replies.

"I don't buy it. We're just nouveau rich in a very temporary sense. I sold my Porsche and I owe a fortune on my co-op apartment. I'd say if we're lucky, after all this settles down, we'll slide back into middle-class."

"If we're lucky?" Patrick says, finding the breath for a short laugh.

"Damn right," I say. "We're going to be out of jobs and racing around New York with resumes identical to thousands of other traders who have no marketable skills anymore."

"I can't tell you how uplifting these early-morning runs are," Patrick says. "You can be such a fucking pessimist."

We run in silence for a while and I think about what Patrick said. Am I a pessimist? I think of myself as a realist. The writing's on the wall and you'd have to be an idiot not to know how to read it. But what about the rest of my life? All the women I've dated since Lydia: never once did I feel optimistic that any of them would turn into a relationship. When it comes to Sara and Florence, I have to say I'm also pretty pessimistic. Neither of them will change her life or make things any better. I basically think that things go the way they've always gone. "An object in motion tends to stay in motion" is my guiding principle.

Have I always been so pessimistic? It's a pretty tough way to go through life. Where did I get this attitude from? I sure didn't inherit it from Mary Ellen, she was an optimist till the last day of her life. She bitched and complained a lot, but she always believed that there was a new adventure waiting for her around the corner. That's the part I don't believe. Actually, belief has nothing to do with it. It's a kind of certainty that pervades my thinking. I feel certain that my career is up in flames, and once that's gone, there won't be another grand opportunity down the road. I hit the high point over the last ten years and all the rest is downhill. Same thing is true with Lydia. She was it; I screwed that up, and again, it goes downhill.

Just what am I optimistic about? I can't think of a damn thing. Except maybe breaking my own running record for speed and distance. In the big picture, not much of a goal.

So why am I not more upset about what was happening at Lambert & Hall and the earthquake through the whole financial world? Odd, I think, in the midst of it all, I find myself strangely calm. Maybe this is the first sign of depression, just basically not caring anymore, letting it all go. But aren't I supposed to go through other stages first like denial and anger? Did I just skip those and go directly to acceptance?

Then I realize what's going on. It's the running. As long as I keep myself moving, eating up the ground under my feet, I can keep the need for adrenaline fixes at bay.

"You want to do the Outer Park Loop?" I ask Patrick, knowing he's already on his last legs.

"No, you go ahead," he says. "I'll just slow you down."

"Okay," I say, giving him a smile as I wave him off. I quickly pick up my pace, cutting out to run the Loop.

This is my drug.

Chapter 30

SARA

SCHOOL STARTED OVER a month ago without me. I was notified in the middle of July that my position had been cut and that I didn't have a teaching contract for the fall semester. At the last minute they tossed me a bone, and offered me the opportunity to substitute teach. I get called about once or twice a week to go in to a classroom where I know none of the children and spend one full day teaching a regimented curriculum that has been left for me. There is no satisfaction in it. The joy of teaching is the relationship that develops with the children, discovering how each one of them learns best, what turns them on. I need a job, so I do it even though the money is terrible.

Peter is out here again and I have to admit I'm so glad to have him around. He arrived last night and he's staying with me again. Maybe he just wants to save the hotel bill but I think it's more than that. I know it has been hard for him since Mother died. I fixed up the guest bedroom for him, so now three of the four bedrooms in my home are occupied.

I'm making raspberry cupcakes this morning. For the last month I've been creating recipes. There are so many little cafés all over West Seattle that have baked goods available. I thought if I could come up with something unique they might be interested in selling them. So far my "Cookies with a Peel" have been a big hit. I put bananas and cinnamon in them. A different twist on chocolate chip cookies. I actually have three little coffee shops buying my cookies regularly. It's probably a ridiculous idea but if I come up with enough new creations, I might be able to have a profitable business.

Peter comes stumbling down the steps. He drinks black coffee while I make him breakfast.

"What's in the oven?" he asks. "It smells terrific in here."

I gave him one of my fresh-baked raspberry cupcakes and share my idea with him. I expect him to laugh it off but he doesn't.

"Cookies with a Peel," he laughs. "I love it, and whatever you put in these cupcakes is fantastic. Don't sell yourself short, Sara, I think you've really got a business here."

"I don't know the first thing about starting a business, Peter. I'm probably not even making any money. The ingredients for all these baked goods most likely cost me as much as I'm charging the cafés for them. At best I'm probably breaking even."

"That's what you've got me for. I'll draw up a business plan for you, help you with marketing," he takes another bite of the cupcake. "This is your talent, Sara. I'm going to help you turn it into gold."

"Well, you do have the Midas touch. You came out of this whole economic mess with at least some of your money intact. If you're serious, Peter, I'd love to try my hand at this."

"How about we sit down this afternoon and put together some ideas?"

"Great. I have about fifteen recipes I've already tested with some of the cafés. Even the Alki Cafe was interested and they do an enormous business."

Peter asks for an update on Florence.

"A lot has changed since your last visit," I tell him.

"Any miracles?" he asks, turning to the financial section of the newspaper.

"She's off her meds again," I say, putting scrambled eggs and bacon in front of him.

"I thought the doctor said if she wasn't taking them she might try the bridge trick again."

"I know. What am I supposed to do?" I want to take the paper away from him and have his full attention.

"Make her take them. Put them in her food," he says nonchalantly, as if he were talking about giving pills to a dog.

"I can't do that," I say

"Why not?" He laughs. "That way at least she won't be paranoid without cause."

"You can't be serious. It would be cruel to trick her that way. She wouldn't know what was happening to her," I respond.

"Better to live like this?" He finally puts down the paper and looks at me.

I decide if this is as good a time as any to tell him. I get him another cup of coffee. "It doesn't matter now. It won't be up to me anymore."

"What does that mean?" he asks. Before I can say anything Florence comes flying through the door. She runs past Peter and me without saying a word and goes up to her room.

"What was that all about?" Peter asks. "What did you mean when you said that it didn't matter now...that it wouldn't be up to you anymore?"

"I'm sending her to a half-way house. I tried to do it a few months ago but I just couldn't. Oh, Peter, what else can I do? She's eating up my life. Do you think I'm a terrible person?"

"No, but you're very good at guilt. Give yourself a break."

"You were right, Peter. I should have done this months ago but I didn't have the heart. I wake up in the middle of the night listening to the walls…hoping that I won't hear her talking to herself. Then I lie there for hours crying. Feeling sorry for her, for myself. Feeling so alone."

"Is this a done deal?" he asks.

"She's leaving on Monday. I'm doing everything you wanted me to in the beginning. I'm letting her go. I'm detaching myself from her."

"It's not what you want?" he says, challenging me.

"I have no choice," I say.

"You do have a choice," he says. "Nine months ago you chose to take care of her here and now you are choosing not to. These are choices."

Florence comes running back down the stairs holding the camera Peter gave her. She starts clicking pictures of Peter and me.

"You want faces," she says. "I can give you faces. Sara says there are no faces in my pictures. You two can be my faces," she says, pushing the camera into Peter's face.

He pushes her away, "Put the camera down."

"Why did you give it to me if you didn't want me to use it? Why do you come here if you don't want to talk to me?"

'Why did you stop taking your pills?" Peter demands of her.

"You don't want to talk. You just want to ask me questions. Make me feel bad. I don't want to feel bad. See, I feel good." Flor-

ence turns on the CD player. "See: music. Come dance with me."
She sings with the music.

"Let's have fun again," she says. "You always come here with a
sour face. Your unhappy face. Do you leave your happy face in New
York? Or maybe you lost it."

Peter switches off the music. "Can you just sit down? You're
making me crazy."

"That's a good one. *I'm* making *you* crazy. Like you have any
idea what crazy is…what it feels like inside my head? Would you
like to come inside my head and see crazy?" She pulls her hair apart
down the middle as if to make an opening in her head. "Here, come
inside."

"Stop it." He pulls her hands away from her head.

His cell phone rings. Florence grabs it and keeps it from him.

"Fine. Take it," he says. "I'm not playing. Be careful with that.
That's got everything in it…my whole brain."

Florence smashes the Blackberry against the counter. Peter tries
to stop her, but the Blackberry is destroyed.

"Damn it," he yells at her.

"Big deal. I smashed your brain. This tiny little thing is so
important to you. Your brain. Go buy another one. *I* can't." Suddenly
Florence stops and begins to cry.

"My brain is smashed too. Broken. Broken. Broken."

"It's not broken. Not if you take the pills," I say.

Florence sits on the floor, weeping. "*Pills*. Pills. I'd rather feel
bad than feel nothing."

I have seen these sudden mood changes many times and maybe
I've grown a little callous to them, but this is the first time Peter has
seen Florence fall apart so completely. He looks shocked. He watches

her for a few moments then gets up and goes to her. Carefully he tries to put his arms around her. At first she pushes him away. Then she lets him hold her.

"I'm sorry," he says, stroking her hair.

"Are you crying?" she says, and I can see that he is.

"Yes," he says softly.

"For me?" she asks.

"Yes."

"Thank you."

Chapter 31

PETER

THE TICKER RUNS across the bottom of the screen. There isn't a broker in New York who is looking at anything other than the ticker. It's October 10th and the stock market has just had its worst week in 75 years. Panic is everywhere. Patrick is hovering over me at my desk.

"This is insane," he says. "Every ten minutes I'm ready to put in a sell order and then the damn thing drops further! This thing has no bottom, Peter."

"We just ride it out and wait for it to turn around," I say.

"And what if it doesn't turn around?" Patrick says. "The Dow is down over 40% since October last year. Not to mention the Standard & Poor's down 18%, its worst week since 1933. The average Joe is losing real money out there, money that's never coming back. Retirement funds are getting decimated."

"So what are you saying here, Patrick? We open up a little surf shop in the Bahamas and watch America become a third-world country?"

"I don't know how you can joke about this, Peter. It could happen. A month from now it could cost $40 for a gallon of milk... the dollar could be worthless. We have to figure out a way to save our asses right now. We can't just sit around and watch Rome burn!"

"They won't let it happen," I say. "The Feds will keep putting a stopper in the drain. Last week they tossed $700 billion to bail out failing banks." Even as I say this I know that we are all just treading water.

When Patrick goes back to his desk, I take my eyes off the ticker and look around the office. The pressure and stress in this room are enough to blow the building. I see Don over in the corner screaming trades into his phone but instead of looking depressed and frightened, he's having the time of his life. He loves the adrenaline rush. That's how the room divides: the guys who feed on this chaos, and those who are crushed by it.

Where do I fit into this picture? I loved the *get* of the deal. I thought about us as warriors going to battle every day. A win meant money in your pocket but more importantly it was a win. I'd gotten to the point where I didn't need more stuff and most of what I had wasn't raising my optimism quotient.

If winning is off the table, what the hell am I doing here anymore?

I don't have an answer, so I take off my tie, put it on my desk, and walk out.

It is surprisingly easy. It just suddenly all looks like a ridiculous game to me. Like we'd been playing with Monopoly money. Tossing around millions like quarters in an arcade. It's a sickness, not to mention corrupt and maybe even illegal. It's as if I had a terrible cancer and now I'm cutting it out of my body. A piece of me will be gone, but the wound will heal back up and I will be healthy again.

I go home and change into my running clothes. The air is that special October crisp and the leaves are all changing in Central Park.

I don't bother stretching. I break into a run, thinking today will be the day I break my record, faster and farther. Ten miles pass quickly in the cloud-covered darkness when a few sprinkles begin to fall. That's fine with me. It'll keep me cool for the next ten miles. I'm doing my own private marathon. The sky could open buckets and it won't stop me. Another couple of miles and little puddles form. My feet make a flapping sound as they hit the dirt.

My mind starts to drift into that trance-like state that clicks in when I'm about twelve miles into a run. I think about Sara and how tough it must be to be a caretaker every day and have no time for your own life. Then my mind drifts to Mary Ellen and, though she drove me crazy, I feel a well of grief, not for me but for her. All her crazy energy, her beautiful voice, gone forever.

My calves and thighs start to burn. I'm pushing them beyond anything they're used to. They are crying out for me to stop. I can't stop. It's not a question of speed or distance anymore. I don't think I can stop running. I just want to go on and on. Run across the bridge, run out of the city.

I think about Florence standing on the edge of that bridge in Seattle last winter, then tossing herself into the freezing water. I had been so cavalier about it at the time. All those years…I was so angry at her. I treated her so badly. I hated her for not getting control of her life and for screwing up mine. I *never* imagined that it wasn't her fault…that she had a real disease, a scary, terrible disease.

It's raining harder now. I keep going. I want the rain to soak through me. I want to feel my skin cold and imagine what Florence must have felt when her body slid under the water and the ice cold of it burned her skin and took her breath away.

My legs no longer feel like they belong to me. They move automatically, disengaged from my brain. I feel pressure in my chest, moving up into my throat. And then it is behind my eyes. I realize that it is not just the rain on my face, but that I am crying. I can't control it. The pressure becomes more and more intense. There are sounds that I realize are coming from me. I am sobbing uncontrollably. I beg my legs to stop, and finally they do. I collapse to the ground exhausted. I am sitting in puddles of rain.

I can't stop crying.

Chapter 32

SARA

HELPED FLORENCE MOVE into a half-way house in mid-October. After checking out at least half a dozen places I decided that Odyssey House was the best. It was small, only fifteen residents, all of them with a diagnosis of schizophrenia. It was just twenty minutes from my house by ferry to Vashon Island.

"It's not a small island," I had told Florence. "There's a nice downtown with lots of little cafés, artist studios and even a movie theater you can go to whenever you like. And it's right on the water. You'll like that. You can walk on the beach."

I had cried for months over the decision to send her away. She fought me right up to the day we moved. I don't know why she was so desperate to stay with me; this couldn't have been a very happy home for her. She was always trying to argue with me, saying that I was too controlling, telling her what to do all the time. She never felt she had any freedom in my house.

When I took her over on the ferry ride to Vashon Island, she warned me that she wouldn't stay a week, she would run away and I would never see her again.

"That's a risk I'll have to take," I told her, trying to be strong and keep it together.

The psychiatrist and Peter had both told me this was the right thing to do. Florence would be able to share what she was going through with other people who had the same disease. Hopefully she would make friends and not feel so desperate and alone. Experienced doctors would carefully monitor her medications to find a balance that would allow her to live as normally as possible while keeping the delusions away. They convinced me that she had a better chance of stabilizing her life at Odyssey House than she did with me. They are only allowing me to visit her once a week.

My house is empty again. Why did I let Roger talk me into buying such a big house? He told me he liked lots of space. I guess what he really wanted was space from *me*. I didn't realize how much I wanted to fill my empty bedrooms. Living alone was not something I chose.

I could sell the house, but in this market it's probably lost half its value. Anyway, I've lived here so long I don't think I'd want to adjust to a new place, a new neighborhood. Everyone knows each other on my block. This is home, a friendly neighborhood. Good people.

I've picked up more substituting jobs, just enough to pay the mortgage and hang on. The district keeps sending out hopeful letters. Teachers may be brought back in January. They even suggest that I may be able to get back my third graders. If not, there's always a Plan B.

Four bedrooms mean I could take in some boarders. It might be fun to have some university students rent rooms in my house. Probably not a realistic idea as the University of Washington is too far from West Seattle for an easy commute. Students won't want to stay here. I would probably get old cranky people and find myself back in the caretaking business.

The truth is I didn't want Florence to leave. As terrible as it could be some days, we still had good moments together. It felt satisfying to be needed again. There was somebody to have coffee with in the morning.

Between substitute teaching jobs, I have a lot of time my hands, so I'm coming up with new baking treats and taking them to the fancy shops in Pikes Market. I can't believe I had the nerve to just walk in with my basketful of cookies and cakes. At first I was afraid they would ask me to leave. Now they greet me at the doors with welcoming smiles, peeking into my baskets to see what I've created.

I'm also back to yoga. The erotic fantasies I had about Sean are gone. They have been replaced by real-life intimacies. I've got another date tonight with Charlie. I have no idea where this is going, if it's going anywhere. At this point I only have two requirements for a relationship and he meets them both: he makes me laugh and he's great in bed. I had forgotten what I was missing all those years.

On one of her more stable days, I told Florence that I slept with Charlie. I had to tell somebody. After five years of celibacy I wanted to celebrate. She was delighted, genuinely happy for me. Then she had a rare moment of openness and told me about Dennis. How much she cared for him and wished that they could have made love together. But the drugs were a wall between them, silencing their libidos.

Charlie will be here any minute and I haven't done my hair yet. And I have to find something bright to wear. Florence has succeeded in changing my wardrobe, so I don't look gray anymore.

Maybe I'll ask Charlie to stay here with me tonight. We usually go to his place. Granted, he lives on the bluff and has a magnificent view of Puget Sound, and I have this old house. But even if it's just for one night, I'd like to not be alone in my own home.

Chapter 33

FLORENCE

'M HERE IN THIS NEW place. Odyssey House they call it, prob-ably because it's where people start their journey into hell. I can't see Sara for a week. I'm alone with strangers. This is my second night here. I keep to myself. There is no one here like Dennis that I can talk to. His words are my mantra: *you can live with the delusions without losing your spirit.* I wish I could believe those words. Most of the time I feel I will never be equal to this illness. There is no way to defeat it. It's stronger than me and it will always win.

Tonight, when the tide is coming in, I walk down to sit on the sea wall watching the water as it comes to me. In the morning I can walk far out on the rocky beach when the tide is low, then at night the water comes creeping back, covering the entire beach. It keeps coming in until there is at least four feet of water against the sea wall, right below my feet.

When the half moon rises in the eastern sky, past and present get mixed up and my mind floats like seaweed on the tide. It gets caught on a piece of driftwood and stops for a while as the water moves around it or maybe it defies the tide and sneaks up in a back eddy. Time isn't a straight line as most people think.

The waves pound against the wall, reaching up to touch my toes.

There is only gray and then black in front of me. I wait for her to come down to me, to join with my body until I am her, the moon once again. Then I can fly away from here into her arms.

But she doesn't come. She has abandoned me. If I can't talk with her, feel her inside me anymore, than who can I be? I call silently to her and still she doesn't come.

I hear a voice, not hers, a new one, inviting me into the sea, offering to come with me as we ride the receding tide far out into the Sound. I wait and listen. It comes again, begging me to become free.

My body moves without my mind. I feel it slip off the sea wall and into the ice-cold water. It surrounds me. I stand on rocks, the water up to my breasts. I take a step forward and the receding tide catches me up. I'm floating.

Then a miracle happens. I see Dennis, just beyond the breakers. He's calling to me, his sweet face smiling at me. I hear his voice whispering, "Are you awake? You're my girl. We're going to help each other make it back."

"Yes, I'm awake," I call to him, my mouth filling with sea water. I can swim to him. Be with him forever. But he's not calling me to him, he's warning me. "Don't," he says. "Go back. It's too cold. Go back."

Suddenly I realize where I am. The tide is pulling me out and this isn't like before. When I flew from the bridge and then swam in the water, it was peaceful and welcoming. I felt safe. I don't feel safe now. I'm terrified. I don't want to drown. With my feet I reach for the sand and rocks beneath me and I can't find them— it's too deep. I look back to the sea wall. How could I be so far out so quickly?

I have to swim back, fight the tide. Fight the pull of the moon.

I kick my legs as hard as I can. Kelp tangles around my arms like snakes holding me, dragging me under. I twist underwater breaking free of the kelp. I will make it to safe ground. I won't let the freezing water have me tonight. I swim back towards the sea wall. There are steps somewhere. I have to fight. My sweater clings to my arms, making them heavy. I push against the tide with every bit of my strength until I'm there on the first step. There is nothing to hang onto, to help me climb, so I drop to my knees and crawl out of the sea.

I'm freezing but I'm alive. I look around to see if anyone has witnessed what happened. No one. I hurry back to my room and quickly change out of my wet, freezing clothes.

Will it happen again? And if it does, will I be able to make it back? The grey night will swallow me and no one will ever know where Florence went. She disappeared into the sky, into the water, and we never found her body.

I'VE BEEN HERE A MONTH now. They have found a new pill that doesn't take all of my Florence-self away. I can go down to the sea wall again…no one calls to me. I walk along the wall every morning. When the tide goes out, seabirds come to pick between the rocks looking for meals. There is a great blue heron that visits every morning. I call him Harry the Heron. He must be almost four feet tall when his neck is extended. Hungry seagulls try to steal his breakfast. When they get too near he chases them away. Yesterday I saw a bald eagle fishing just beyond the point. They tell me in the springtime there's a nesting pair of eagles in the tree just behind Odyssey House. I'd like to see them, but I hope I'm not here in the spring.

I thought I would hate this place, that it would just be like the hospital. But here all the doors are unlocked. They call us residents and not patients. We are free to go where we want on the island. There aren't a lot of rules. Our medications are monitored carefully. There are daily group sessions and meetings individually with our therapists. The rest of the time is our own.

AFTER TWO MONTHS THE psychiatrist decides that I am doing better. It's up to me if I want to stay longer or go back home to Sara's. The other residents have been at Odyssey House for six months to three years. Their families want them to stay here. I guess it's just too hard to have us in their homes. We disrupt their lives and embarrass them. Probably Sara feels that way too. But I miss her. She is all the family I have, and I want to go home.

Sometimes I still hear the moon calling me. I listen without responding.

I hold two realities in my head: the world that comes from inside me, and the world outside me. And they are equally real.

I live precariously between these two worlds.

Chapter 34

PETER

FOR ONCE IT'S NOT POURING when I touch down in
Seattle. It's a rare clear day for December. On our descent the
pilot announces that our flight path takes us right over Mount
Rainer's snow-covered peak, so we can enjoy a sight that is hidden
most of the winter. I feel like I'm above Mount Everest, looking
down at the top of the world. We are so close to the summit as we
approach that I can actually see flags that were planted last summer
by climbers who made it to the top. There is a collective silence in
the plane as we all experience the grandeur of this moment.

I get a cab at the airport and head to a hotel downtown. Sara
doesn't know I'm coming in. I need a couple of days to myself before
I call her.

Colored lights and decorations are up all along Pike Place
Market and the Wharf. Christmas has always been an annoyance
for me at best. Investors I needed to get to were on vacation. Our
offices were closed. I couldn't wait for the New Year to begin and
the lost two weeks of Christmas to be over. So what was it going to
feel like now, I thought, when I had no investors, or anything else
for that matter, to get back to?

The Marquis Hotel is just blocks from the water and my room

has a great view over the Sound. I had decided to splurge. What the hell, I am maybe one of the few guys who got out with my resources still largely intact.

For the last two months, since the day of my personal meltdown in Central Park, I had been cleaning up my life. Homes all over America were going into foreclosure, but New York real estate was still at a premium. I had managed to sell the loft for pretty much what I had paid for it. I had liquidated most of my stock positions before the big crash in October, so even though I lost a bundle I still had a nice nest egg sitting safely in Certificates of Deposit. What seemed like a lifetime of living and breathing Wall Street was pretty much wrapped up in that brief two months.

The last thing I did before flying out was to rent a car and drive up to Connecticut. I went to the cemetery where Mary Ellen was buried. I dusted the snow off of the stone we had placed there for her. Sara wasn't happy with the inscription I had insisted on putting on the stone that would mark Mary Ellen's grave. Sara wanted it to say something traditional, like beloved mother and wife. Those words could never define Mary Ellen or hold the vast extent of her personality. She was unique and I wanted her stone to reflect that.

In spite of the foot of snow that had fallen recently, relatives had still come to put flowers on grave sites. Maybe I should have done that, but then she never wanted flowers in vases when she was alive. Mother wanted flowers in the ground, growing and alive. She wanted books, music, and adventures.

I read the five simple words I had inscribed on the stone:

I Did It My Way.

Perfect. It was exactly what she would have wanted.

Well, Mom, this is it, I had said. Our last goodbye. If you were alive you would tell me I was nuts for just walking away from it all. You would tell me that I was a coward, that I'd lost my nerve, that New York was going to come back and I should stay here and come back with it. You would be wrong.

THERE REALLY ISN'T THAT much I have to do before telling Sara I am here. I'll open a few bank accounts, move money, have lunch with the few referrals I picked up before leaving New York. Make a few connections, put out feelers. Basically I want to have some time to walk around the town. That's what I had done when I first got to New York. I walked all over the city until it became my home. Seattle is going to be a lot harder to possess. That's why I wanted to start downtown. Sara lives only fifteen minutes away in West Seattle, but it feels so much further. It's something about the bridge I have to cross to get into West Seattle; it makes it a suburb, an appendage, away from the action. I'm a downtown guy, maybe. Maybe not, anymore.

I HAVE NO IDEA HOW SARA is going to react to my proposal. I guess this is the day to find out. She is completely caught off guard when I call her and tell her I'm in Seattle and that I'm coming over tonight. I'm surprised when she tells me, no, that she's busy tonight. She has a date. My sister has a date!

"Tomorrow would be better. Can you come over around noon?" she says. "Florence will be here by then so you'll get to see her. She's coming over on the ferry for a visit."

"How about I get there around ten so that we can talk before

Florence arrives?" I suggest.

I arrive the next morning to find Sara in an upbeat mood. She seems genuinely glad to see me but I can tell she is preoccupied. We have coffee together over a guarded conversation. She wants to know what I'm doing here now and why I didn't call sooner and I want to know whether she is finally having some kind of sex life. Neither one of us is ready for full disclosure. It takes me a while to work up to revealing my plan.

"Two months ago you told me you might open the house to boarders because you could use the money. So here's an idea. What if I come live with you? You can overcharge me for the rent."

"You can't be serious," Sara says. I know this hits her from out of the blue.

"You've got empty bedrooms," I say, as if this simple fact makes my case by itself.

"No!" she says, without thinking about it. "You can't just show up and expect me to open my arms...my house to you." I'm surprised by her strong reaction. I'm also impressed.

"I thought you would be happy," I say apologetically.

"Happy. Why? So I could have another person to take care of?"

"I don't need taking care of."

"You plan to get a job? Live here permanently?" she interrogates me.

"I don't have plans. It's just an idea."

"No, this is all wrong. Go back to New York," she says. "I'm doing fine now. I don't need your money. *Sara's Sweets* really took off. Peter, you can't believe how well I'm doing. The phone is ringing off the hook with shops and cafes ordering my cookies and cakes."

"That's terrific," I say.

"I never could have done it without you," she admits.

"If I'm here we can bring Florence back home," I try again to make my case. "I'll help take care of her. Start over here. She's ready to live here again. We can't leave her in a half-way house forever… if we do she may never be able to live on her own. I want to help. I *need* to help. This is it. We're family."

"How can three adult siblings living together be healthy?" Sara asks. There is a moment of silence, and then we both laugh.

"Anything is possible," I say. "Look, this isn't meant to be a permanent arrangement. How about we just start with a month…a little month? We see how it goes. We take one step at a time."

"I have a man in my life." She says. There's not just happiness but pride in her voice.

"Good. I'm happy for you," I say sincerely. "My being here is only going to help. You can go out with him while I'm here with Florence."

Sara tosses the last of her coffee into the sink. "I don't know if Florence should come back here."

"It's your decision. Whatever you want," I say. "It's your house, your life. I defer to you."

"I don't need you," she says with a quiet clarity. And I see that it's true.

"I know," I say. "But *I* need *us*, the three of us."

"You have no idea how hard this is," she says.

"You're right, I don't. But maybe it won't be so hard if we do it together. It's your choice. The half-way house may still be the better decision."

"Why…why would you choose this?" Sara looks at me as if I'm

someone she doesn't know and is trying to figure out.

"It chose us. It's the journey we're on now. She needs us both."

"What if we aren't enough?" she says. "What if it never gets any better? What if—"

"Too many what ifs," I say, taking Sara's hand. "What if we just try it? Give her a family."

"Peter, you're having a career meltdown. In a month you'll want to go home …back to New York."

"No, I don't think so. Florence can always move back to the half-way house at any point if it gets too tough."

"It was already too tough," Sara says.

WE PICK FLORENCE UP AT the ferry terminal at noon. Her face is wind-blown red from standing on the deck during the short crossing. I think I see the slightest smile when she sees me. We take her home in silence. She doesn't ask why I'm here. Sara makes us a simple lunch, ham and cheese sandwiches.

I ask Florence how she's doing. She responds with single-words answers.

"Florence, come here," I say carefully. "We have something to tell you."

She looks at me, waiting, and I am silent. The right words aren't coming to me. If she hates this idea, I don't know what I'll do. She has to want me here, not just tolerate me, like I tolerated her when she lived with me. This has to be the right choice for all three of us.

Sara sees that I'm afraid of Florence's response. She jumps in and says it so simply. "Peter is staying here. He's not going back to New York. "

Florence is puzzled. "You're going to live here? Take my

place?"

"No one can take your place here," I say. "How about if we both stay here for a while? Only if that's okay with you."

"I don't have to go back to the Odyssey House?"

"Not today."

"Some day?" she asks.

"I don't know. Maybe," I admit. "I left my job."

"Was that hard?" Florence asks.

"No, that wasn't the hard part," I say.

"What was the hard part?" Her question is simple and direct.

"Leaving Mother," I say, realizing the truth of it even as I say it out loud.

"But she's dead. Isn't she still dead?"

"I know she's dead, Florence. It's the habit of going to visit her, bringing her things. She's not there any more but I still feel like I'll be betraying her by leaving."

"You don't have to leave her," Florence gives me a wide smile. "I keep Dennis with me all the time."

"So, Florence, do you want me here?" I ask.

"Did you forget it rains ten months of the year? It gets dark, too, in the winter. Dark all day," she says.

"It's winter now. We'll go into the dark together," I say.

"What if Sara marries Charlie?" she asks.

"I've only been seeing him for two months," Sara laughs.

"Let's deal with the present," I say. "This moment. Isn't that what you told us? You wanted to find a *still point* when everything was quiet, even if just for a minute."

I pick up the camera I gave Florence. I set it on an end table facing the sofa where Sara and Florence are sitting.

"Let's be still for one minute," I say.

I push the self-timer button and run to the sofa to sit between my sisters. We all look straight into the camera and freeze. The flash goes off.

Together we look at the photo in the camera. Our family portrait.

We aren't smiling, but there is a shine of hope on all our faces.

· ·

ACKNOWLEDGEMENTS

The friends of writers must frequently be put in the awkward position of reading and commenting on a work in progress. The trick is to select brave honest friends and fellow writers whose opinions you trust and respect. Fortunately I have found not only support and encouragement but excellent readers and critics. The first of these is, of course, my husband, Marc, who is continually subjected to my requests for feedback. Throughout our almost thirty-year marriage, he has stoically endured my habit of having few unexpressed thoughts. I could do very little without his love, his patience, his amazing sense of humor and his keen intellect.

My dear friends Tom Weingarten and Wendy Thon, who live in West Seattle and are the reasons I spend so much time in the Pacific Northwest, followed my narrative across every bridge and waterway, helping me keep my world authentic. Their editorial savior-faire made them invaluable readers. Elizabeth Clark-Stern gave me an early draft of her own novel, *Safari to Mara*, and her fine writing inspired me to find my voice again. My witty friend Sandra Tsing Loh, who has read everything I've written at least twice, gave me the benefit of her own unique vision. Nanci Hendrickson tactfully made me rethink much of the early flow of the novel. Bev Kaye and Barry Levitt, my business partners and friends for a quarter century, read the final draft and gave me encouragement and endless support. Christine Kruttschnitt, U.S. Correspondent for Germany's *Stern* Magazine, graciously offered her insights. And thank you to my wonderful friends Jackie Petras, Ed Martin, Kathy Bates, Marcia Heinegg, Sharon & Noel Webb, Barry Bortnick, Susan Edlinger and Carol & Dan Orsborn, who continue to get me through tough times.

Linda Roghaar, my publisher, provided enthusiasm and excellent advice from our first conversation. It was a pleasure working with her and her team.

And, most of all, thank you to everyone who is reading this novel and sharing this journey with me.

An Interview with Beverly Olevin

What first inspired you to write The Good Side of Bad?

I think I was more compelled to write this novel than inspired. I wanted to discover how people react when confronted with a turn of events that tosses their lives in unexpected and challenging directions. When the once reasonably predictable future becomes a chaos of ambiguity or loss, how do we find the courage and resilience to adapt? I created three characters, siblings, who were all forced by external events to face major changes in their lives. My hope was that I could give these siblings, whose lives and challenges are very different, ways to find a path towards each other.

My own life had suddenly and dramatically changed as a result of an illness, and I found writing this book was my own life raft to survival and coming to terms with "life interrupted." The greatest satisfaction and even joy in writing for me comes when the characters I have created slowly become so real to me that they are capable of making their own choices, continually surprising and teaching me in the process.

Which of the three main characters came to you first?

The character of Florence was based on a woman in her mid-twenties I knew many years ago. I was haunted by how her young life was forever altered by mental illness. I had worked in a psychiatric half-way house for a short time when I was younger, so I had compassion for what she was going though.

I wanted to juxtapose Florence's terrifying mental breakdown with a character at the other extreme of life. A New York hedge fund trader was about as far as I could get from Florence's life. I had closely followed the economic events of 2008 and wanted to explore what happened to a high-flying trader when his world melted down...so Peter was born.

At first I wanted Sara to be a place of calm amidst the chaos her brother and sister were facing. But I could hardly leave her as passive glue in the middle of other people's lives. In the end, the changes and choices of her life were as powerful for me as those of her more dramatic siblings.

Why did you choose to write the novel from three first-person voices?

In an early draft the novel was in the third person. Most of my short stories and my novel, *The Breath of Juno*, were written in the third person. As a playwright, I love the free flow of creating dialogue. I love hearing characters' voices in novels; it's a great way of getting their unique personality on the page. But for this book it didn't feel like that was enough. I think it is almost impossible to understand what a person like my character of Florence is going through without being inside her head. A third person narrative couldn't touch the depth of her struggle. She had to be the narrator of her own life. As soon as I put her voice on the page, I knew that Peter and Sara needed to speak for themselves as well.

Writing from the first person, especially in three different voices, was, at first, so much harder than having the all-knowing perspective of the third person voice. But it was so much more intimate to me.

You make several life and death decisions. Did you know which way these choices would go at the beginning?

I never know how everything will go. That's the thrill of writing a novel. I start with a chapter by chapter outline but I never stick to it.

Sometimes a single sentence will force the book to go in a different direction. At first the fate of my characters is all in my hands. If I'm their creator, I believe I can make them do whatever I like, but that doesn't last long. Even at the very end there were choices that were made, not in my head in advance, but in the midst of the action.

I'm reluctant to say anything more about these choices. I don't want to spoil it for those who might read this interview before starting the book.

The story is set mostly in Seattle and New York. The financial Wall Street plot clearly dictates the New York location. But why Seattle?

I live in Los Angeles, but all my summers for the past fifteen years have been spent in the Pacific Northwest. The beauty and the water draw me there with every summer solstice. Seattle is surrounded by water with Puget Sound on one side and Lake Washington on the other. Bridges cross over small canals and vast lakes. Everywhere the water is waiting, tempting, inviting. Water literally runs through the novel. And there is the ever-present rain.

Seattle is also about as far as you can get from the New York world of high finance, at least geographically.

What do you hope readers will take away from the story?

All of the characters are on their own journey towards understanding and compassion. I guess that is the one thing I would want readers to feel. When people come to a crossroads in their lives, they not only discover who is there to fight with them but how they ultimately learn to find the strength to fight for themselves. Our motivations, our choices and even our values can be wildly different, but opening yourself to deeply knowing someone can't help but bring compassion.

....

About the Author

Beverly Olevin's last novel was *The Breath of Juno*. Her short fiction has been published in literary magazines across the country. She is also a playwright and theater director. In 2008 she was Artist-in-Residence for the UCLA Osher Lifelong Learning Institute. She teaches courses in acting and theatre at UCLA and University of Washington. Beverly's non–fiction publications have sold worldwide. She has an undergraduate degree from UCLA and an MFA from Trinity University. She lives in Los Angeles with her husband Marc and her border collie Sadie.

For Reading Group topics and Discussion Questions please visit the author's website for more information:

www.beverlyolevin.com

CPSIA information can be obtained at www.ICGtesting.com
Printed in the USA
LVOW07s2013220915

455249LV00001B/145/P